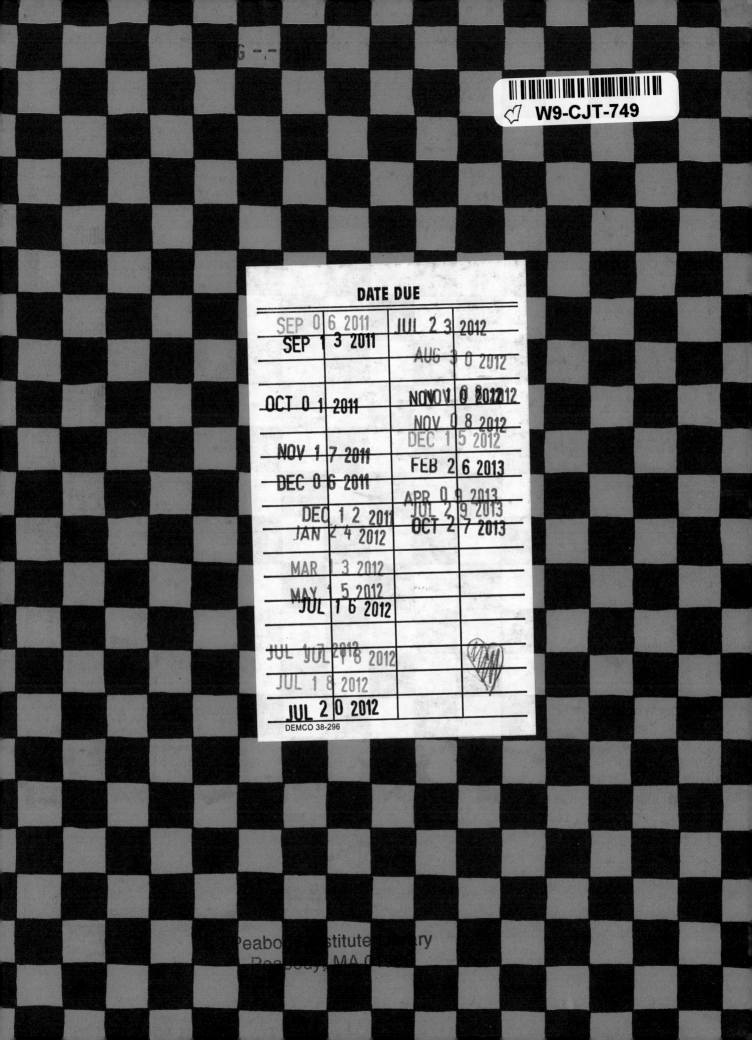

SCARY GODMOTHER™

written and illustrated by

JILL THOMPSON

Dark Horse Books®

President & Publisher
Mike Richardson

Editor
Sierra Hahn

Assistant Editor
Freddye Lins

Collection Designer
Tina Alessi

Special thanks to Scott Allie and John Schork.

SCARY GODMOTHER™

This volume reprints the storybooks *Scary Godmother*; *Scary Godmother: The Revenge of Jimmy*; *Scary Godmother: The Mystery Date*; *and Scary Godmother: The Boo Flu* (originally published by Sirius Entertainment, Inc.); as well as the short story "Tea for Orson" from *Trilogy Tour II*.

Published by Dark Horse Books
A division of Dark Horse Comics, Inc.
10956 SE Main Street
Milwaukie, OR 97222

darkhorse.com

To find a comics shop in your area, call the Comic Shop Locator Service toll-free at (888) 266-4226.

First edition: October 2010
ISBN 978-1-59582-589-6

3 5 7 9 10 8 6 4 2
Printed by Midas Printing International, Ltd., Huizhou, China.

this book is dedicated to...

ISLA-SOPHIA

The Stories

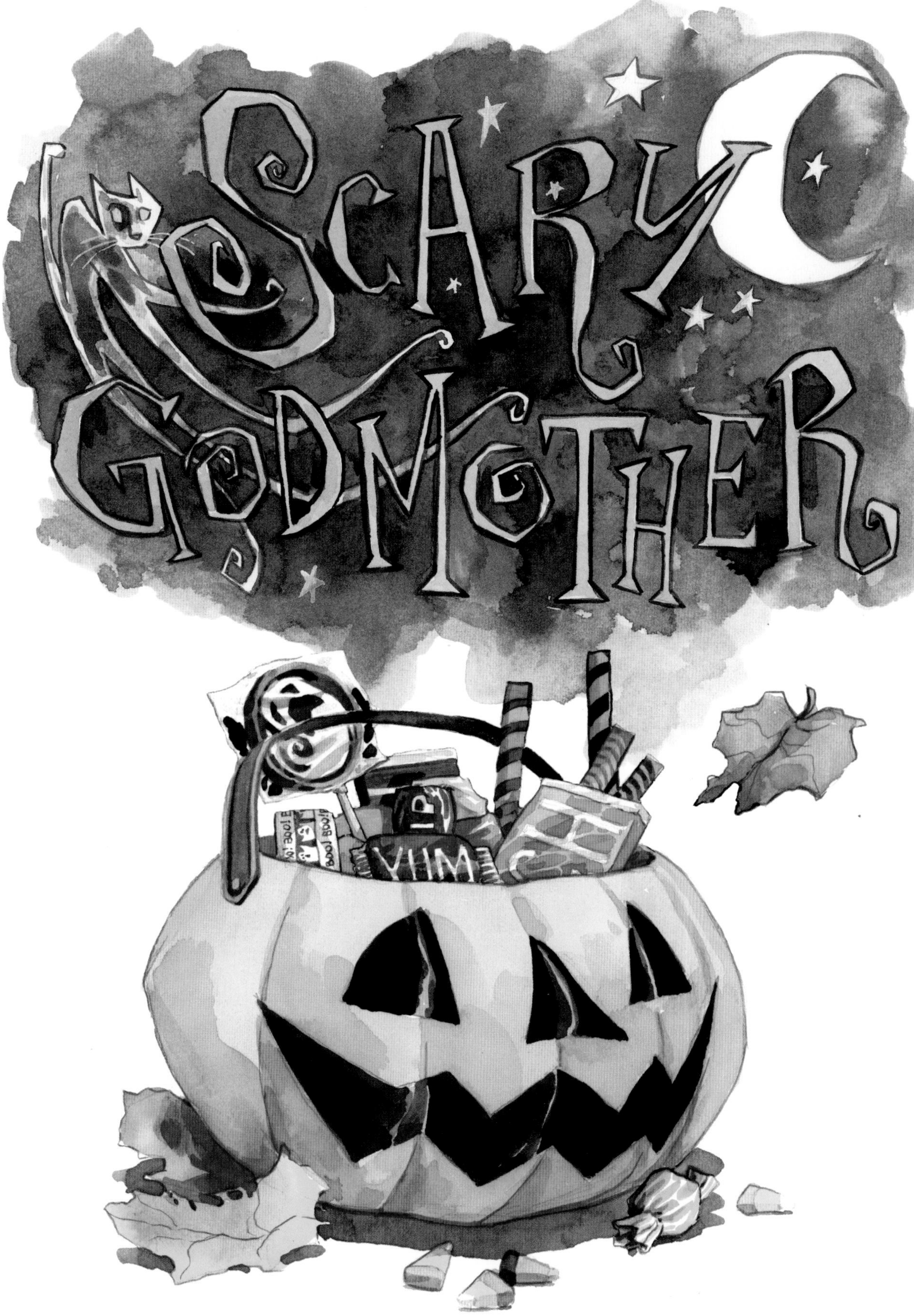
SCARY
GODMOTHER

It was probably the most exceptional Halloween night ever. The warm wind smelled softly of burning jack-o'-lanterns and dry leaves as it pushed clouds across the rapidly darkening sky. All of this made Hannah Marie excited and impatient.

Tonight was the very first time Hannah would go trick-or-treating without her parents. She was going to go with the big kids. Her grandmother helped make her fairy princess costume with sequins on the wings. She even had a plastic pumpkin to hold her treats in.

Hannah was afraid of monsters—especially tonight. She was worried they would try to get her while she was trick-or-treating. Monsters abound on Halloween!

Just then, the doorbell rang! It was her older cousin, Jimmy, and his friends Daryl, Bert, and Katie. They had come to take her trick-or-treating with them. No monsters would dare touch her as long as she was with her cousin. He was big and a real scrapper!

A curfew was set before Hannah was allowed to leave.

Hannah kissed her mom and dad goodbye and then ran down the sidewalk after the older children. Her first Halloween as a "big kid" had begun!

Jimmy whispered to his friends so Hannah and her parents couldn't hear.

Hannah's legs were much shorter than the others, and she had to run sometimes to keep up with them. The big kids had to stop many times to wait for her.

Jimmy wished that his cousin wasn't with them.

They trick-or-treated down the whole block.

At house after house, their neighbors admired their costumes and loaded their bags with goodies.

It was hard for Hannah to get up and down the stairs, so Daryl, Bert, and Katie stopped to help her. Not Jimmy, though. He just stood by himself and grumbled.

Suddenly, an idea popped into his head.

A nasty idea.

If Hannah got scared she'd *want* to go home. It would be her *idea* and I wouldn't get in *any* trouble.

A nasty, mean, selfish, and devilish idea.

Then we'd be free to go to a *million* more houses and get a *bazillion* more pieces of candy...

While they marched onward, Jimmy filled the others in on his plans for Hannah. She followed behind, unaware that a very rotten trick was about to be played on her.

Soon they were walking down a street Hannah had never been on before. She thought about using her flashlight, but she trusted Jimmy and figured he'd protect her . . .

Further down the mysterious street they passed an old cemetery.
Hannah was sure she saw a monster hiding in the weeds!

And even though her head was telling her to go home, her feet raced forward through
the piles of leaves and down the crooked sidewalk to catch up with the others.

She finally caught up with them at the end of the street—the dead end! Jimmy and the others were peering around a big old tree at the creepiest house she had ever seen! Why had they stopped here, of all places?

Jimmy made up a story he was certain would frighten his cousin all the way back home.

The big kids giggled and anxiously waited for their trick to work . . .
But much to everyone's surprise . . .

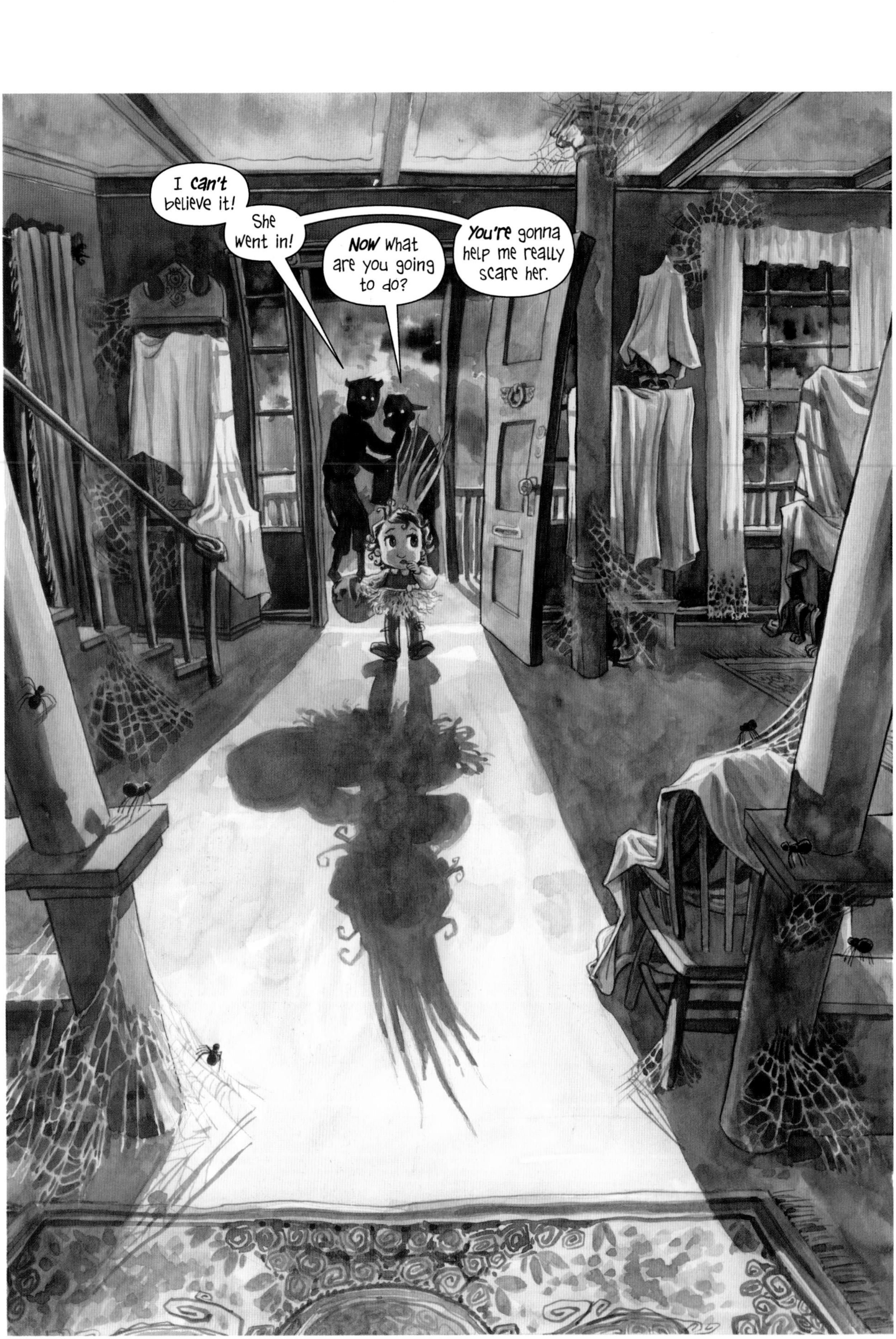
I **can't** believe it!
She went in!
NOW what are you going to do?
You're gonna help me really scare her.

They tiptoed through the dark, dusty house. Jimmy pointed out imaginary monsters amongst the antiques, and the others played along.

Hannah's belly bubbled with fear as she followed them deeper and deeper into the house. She never knew being a big kid was so scary! Once she left some candy on the steps, they could leave.

The **Monster** in the Basement! Hannah closed her eyes,
and threw some candy down the long, dark stairs.

When she opened her eyes, she found herself **alone**—in the **dark**—with the **Monsters**. The
kids were gone! Had the Monsters gobbled them up? But why? She had given them candy . . .

She tried to be brave, but she couldn't hold out any longer. Hannah began to cry.

When, suddenly, out of the darkness came the sound of sobbing—much louder than her own!

Why would anybody be crying louder than a little girl left alone in a Spook House?
Hannah choked back her tears and decided to find out.

The witchy lady bent down and laughed. She extended her hand and smiled big and wide!

Hannah Marie shook the long, bony fingers that wiggled in front of her.

With a big laugh and a great smile, Hannah's Scary Godmother flapped her little bat wings and whisked them up the attic stairs to the top of the house!

The Scary Godmother knock-knock-knocked on the attic door.
Wait a minute—nobody lived in the attic—did they?

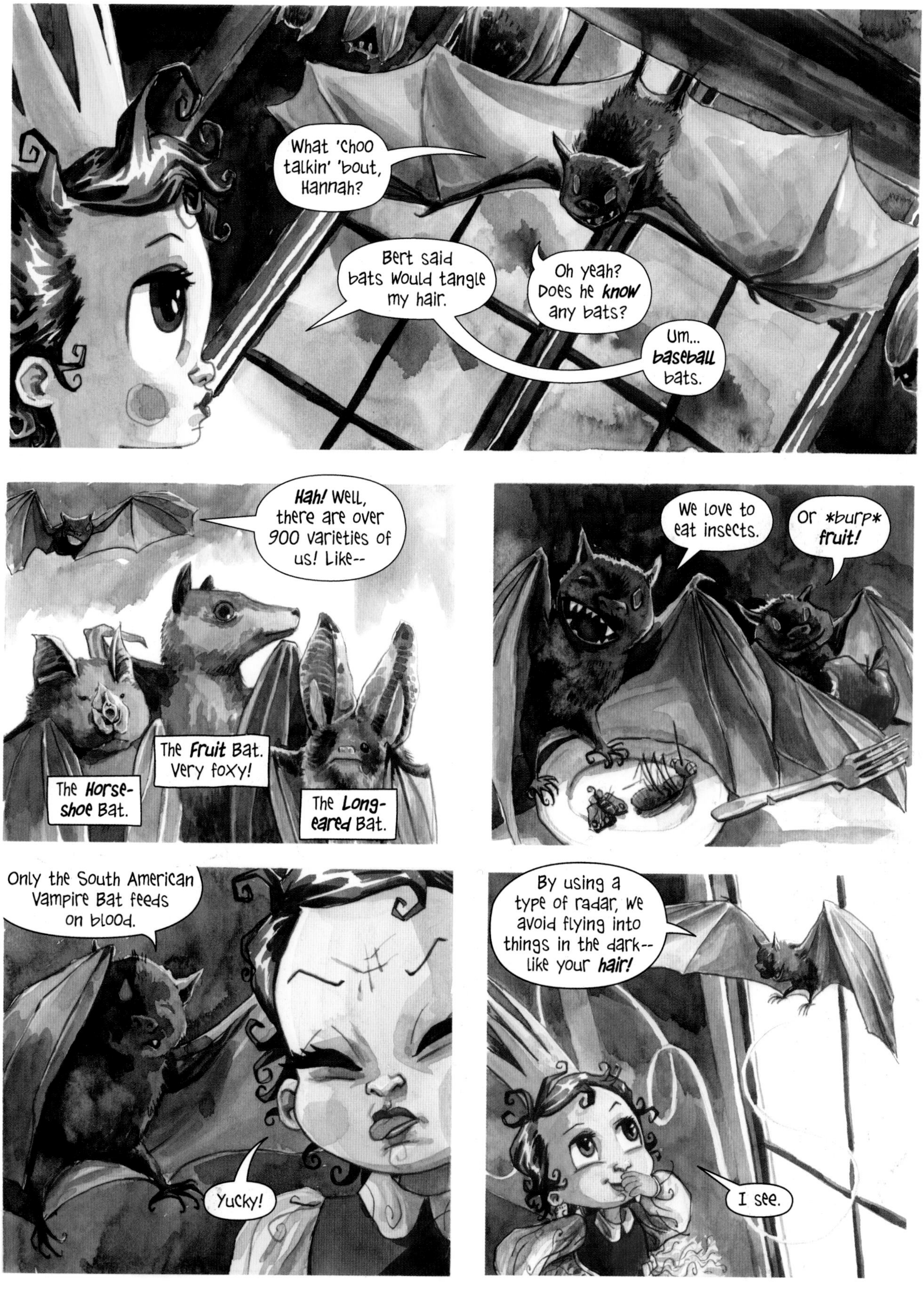
What 'choo talkin' 'bout, Hannah?
Bert said bats would tangle my hair.
Oh yeah? Does he **know** any bats?
Um... **baseball** bats.
Hah! Well, there are over 900 varieties of us! Like--
The **Horse-shoe** Bat.
The **Fruit** Bat. Very foxy!
The **Long-eared** Bat.
We love to eat insects.
Or *burp* **fruit!**
Only the South American Vampire Bat feeds on blood.
Yucky!
By using a type of radar, we avoid flying into things in the dark-- like your **hair!**
I see.

Having learned a bit about bats, the Scary Godmother then flew Hannah down the stairs, where she began knock-knock-knocking on the closet doors. Who could she be looking for?

Suddenly, a skeleton clacked out of the armoire behind them!

It was Skully Pettibone, a friend of Scary Godmother's! He worked in the closets
of all of the old houses, keeping their secrets and occasionally rattling around.
He sang the bone song while Hannah jumped up and down on the bed!

Their laughter woke Boozle, the Scary Godmother's Scaredy Cat, who rose out from
under the bed to see what the commotion was all about. And before she knew it, Hannah
Marie was a little girl who was no longer afraid of bats, ghosts, or clackety bones!

Then a gruff voice piped up from a heating vent down below.

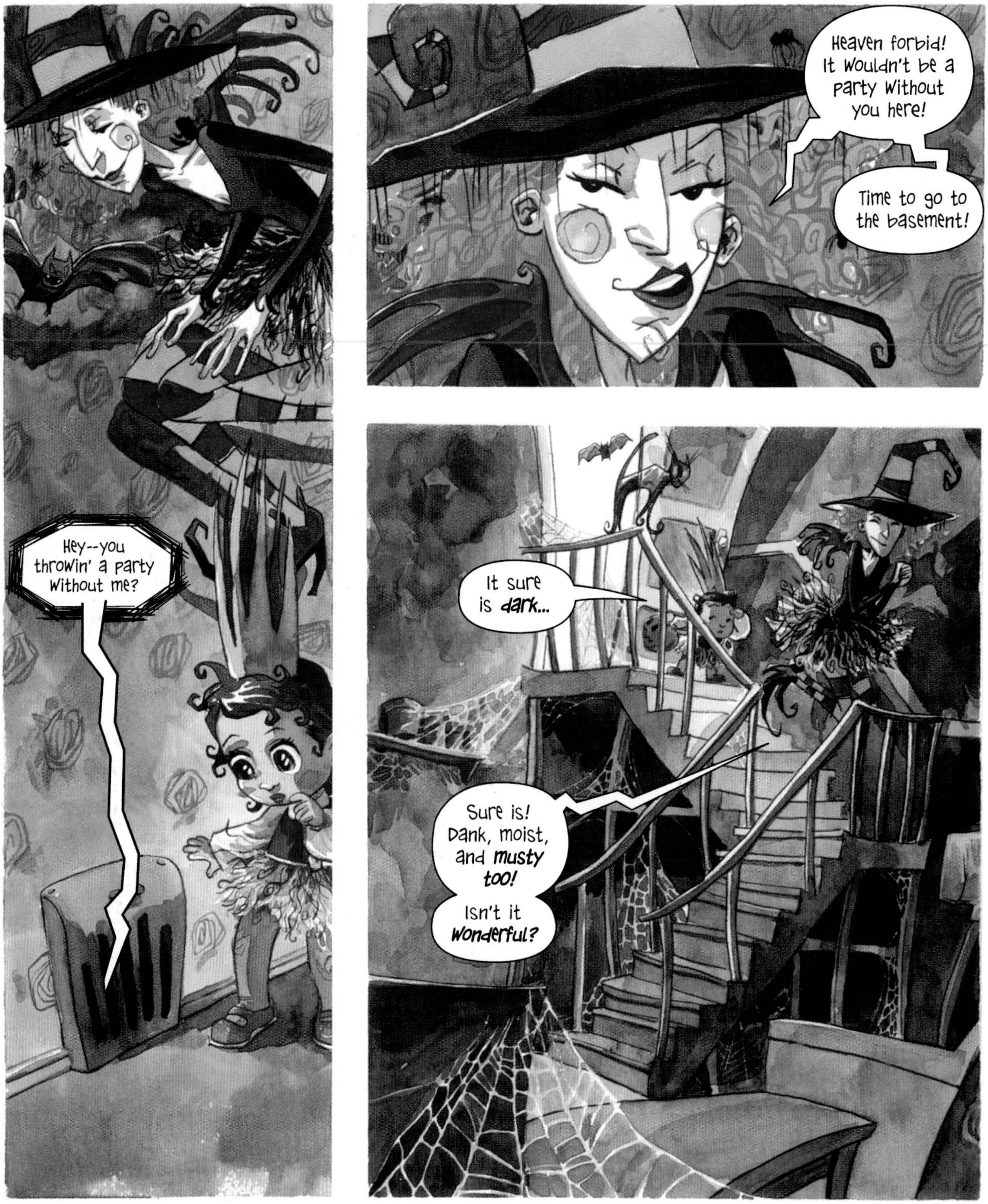
Hey--you throwin' a party without me?
Heaven forbid! It wouldn't be a party without you here!
Time to go to the basement!
It sure is dark...
Sure is! Dank, moist, and musty too!
Isn't it wonderful?

They all made their way down the creaky stairs.
So, Hannah was finally going to meet the **Monster** in the Basement!

From out of the darkness under the stairs, glittering eyes popped out at them.

A Monster with horns, and fur, and claws shambled into the dim light of the basement. Its yellow eyes gleamed as it observed Hannah, and a wide, toothy mouth cut its face into a grin!

Remembering what Jimmy had told her, Hannah reached into
her jack-o'-lantern and pulled out a candy to offer the beast.

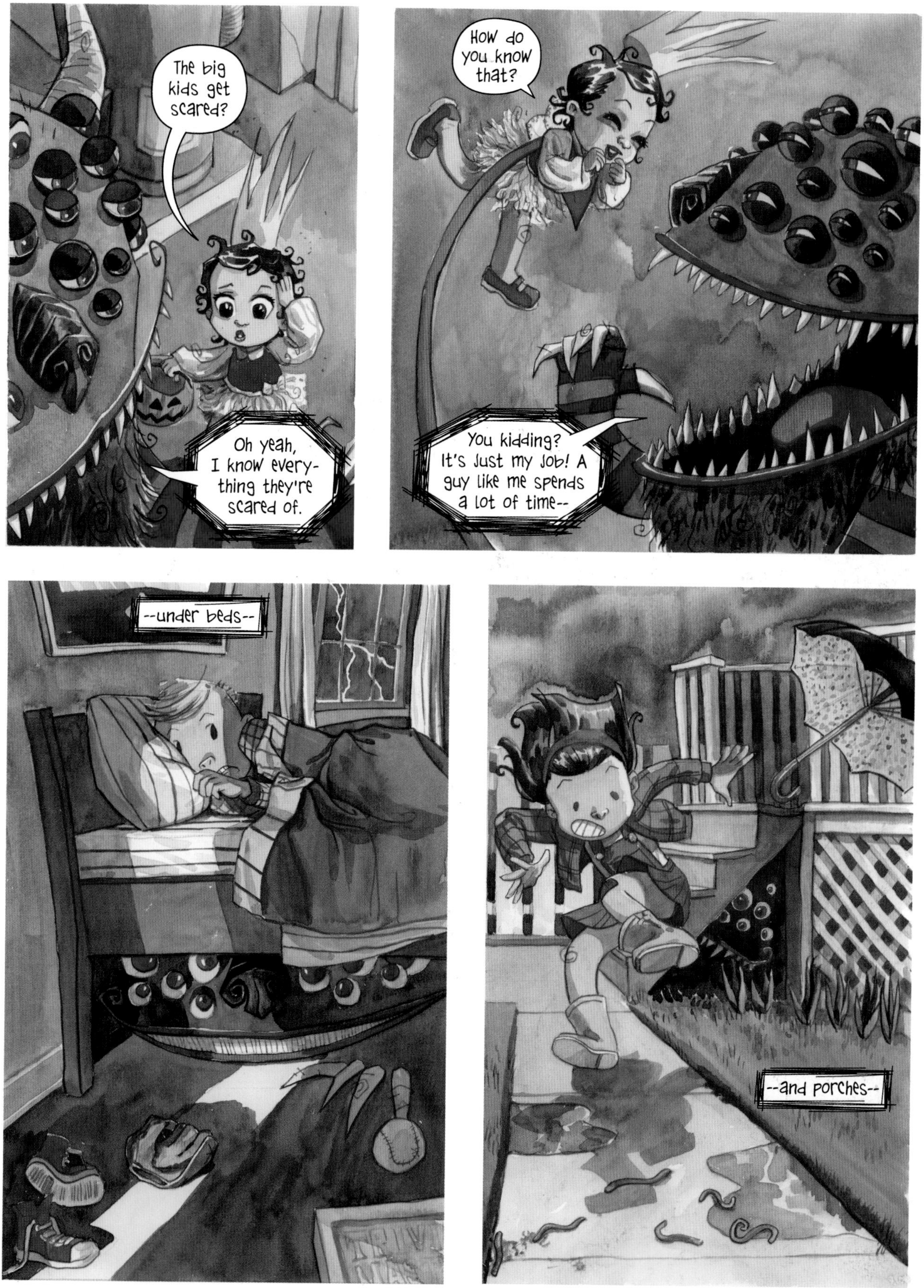
The big kids get scared?
Oh yeah, I know every-thing they're scared of.
How do you know that?
You kidding? It's just my job! A guy like me spends a lot of time--
--under beds--
--and porches--

--and in closets--

--and in crevices. You might say I know the secret things that everyone's afraid of!

And right now, it's no secret those kids are afraid of being punished! Listen!

Why did I listen to you! I'm gonna get *grounded* for sure!

I can't believe we left the *baby* in the *SPOOK House!*

My Mom's gonna whup my butt!

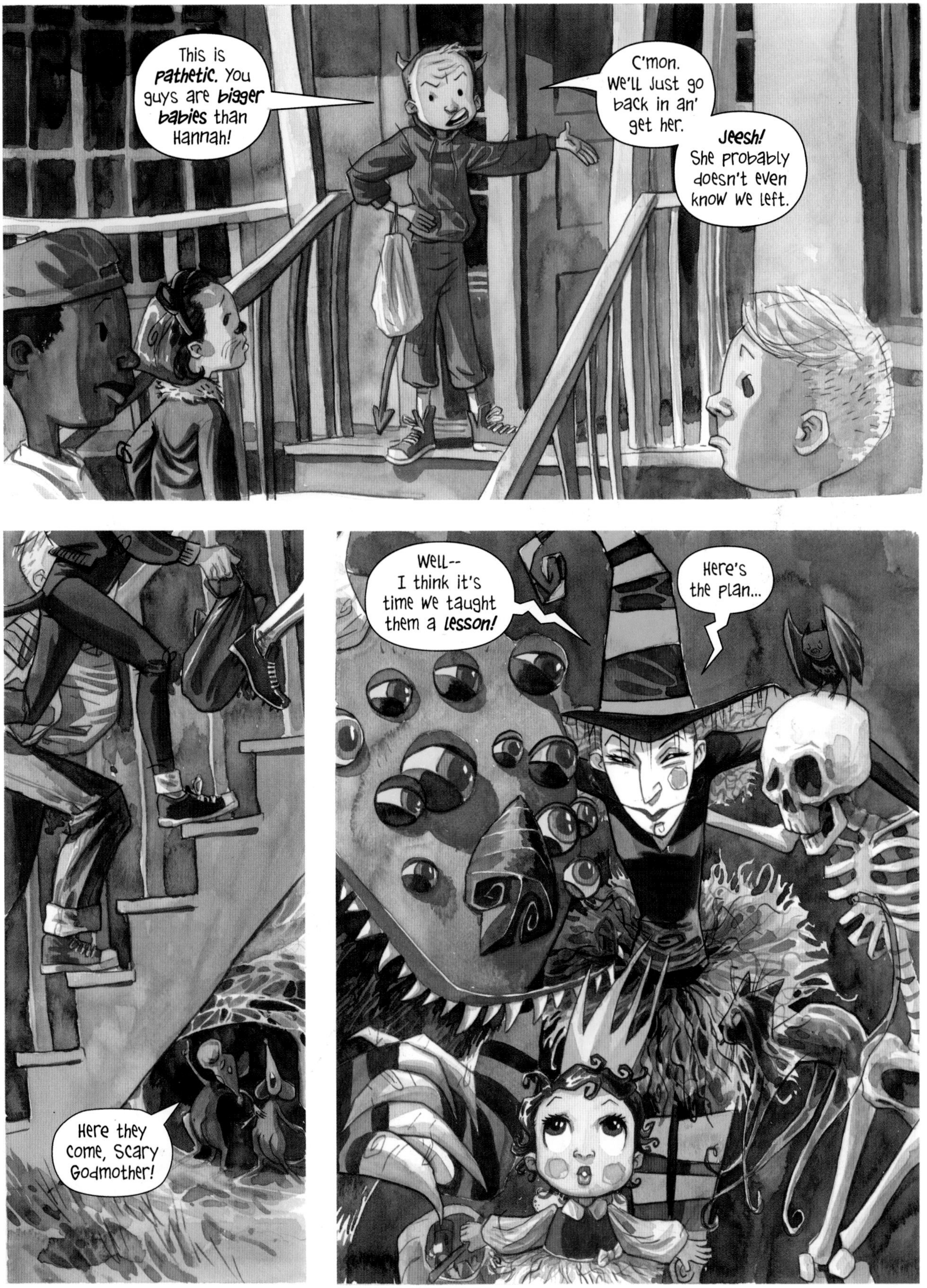
This is pathetic. You guys are bigger babies than Hannah!
C'mon. We'll just go back in an' get her.
Jeesh! She probably doesn't even know we left.
Here they come, Scary Godmother!
Well-- I think it's time we taught them a lesson!
Here's the plan...

They warily crept back into the house, unaware that a Skeletal presence was spying on them.

Skully Pettibone clattered his bones with all the muscle-free might he could muster!

They scrambled away from the creature's bony grasp, but it rattled closer and closer . . .

Too late! A great, ghostly beast let out a chilling "Meeooow" and blocked their way!
They had no choice but to run deeper into the house!

A squadron of bats dove upon them and into the living room! Closing their eyes, they clamored screaming towards the kitchen, as the bats creepily squeaked in laughter.

Cornered! This was it . . . There was nowhere left to go but . . . the Basement!

The door slammed shut! Now they were alone . . . in the dark!

Then there was a rumbling—**no**, it was **growling**, deep and throaty, seeping out of the inky darkness behind them. Then they felt a breezy draft— **no**, it was **steamy**, **hot breath**, **huffing** and **puffing** down on their necks!

There **really** was a Monster in the Basement!

It was coming for them, licking its thick lips and baring its pointy teeth.

The Monster was going to gobble them up!

Suddenly—the Monster **screamed**!

It wiggled and jiggled on the floor, trying to escape from the bright beam of light!

Then—poof! It vanished in a puff of acrid smoke! Pee-yeeew!

They were **saved**! What brave-hearted **hero** had bested the toothy horror?
A policeman or parents for sure! Looking up at the stairs, who do you think they saw?

Jimmy was **so** scared he tumbled up the stairs and **over** the others!

Hannah **bravely** led the way out of the house that was now **crawling** with **spooks**!
The beam of her light kept the creatures at bay.

Protected by Hannah and her flashlight, the big kids ran howling out of the front door—
leaving **all** of their **trick-or-treat** candy behind!

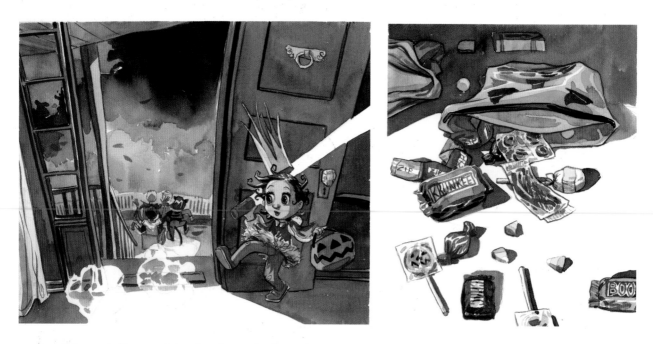

Hannah lingered in the doorway for a few moments with her new Halloween friends.

Hannah thanked them, one by one.

And she ran out the door into the pumpkiny air and bright moonlight.

The kids **promised** to make up for being so mean to her.
When Jimmy delivered her home—at exactly eight o' clock—her **jack-o'-lantern**
was over.flowing with Halloween favors from the best trick-or-treat houses!

Later that night, tucked snug in her bed, Hannah thought of spooky things while drifting off to sleep. She couldn't wait until next Halloween when she could see the ghosts, and monsters, and her Scary Godmother, again!

Maybe tonight, if she was lucky, she would have a really scary dream . . .

THE END

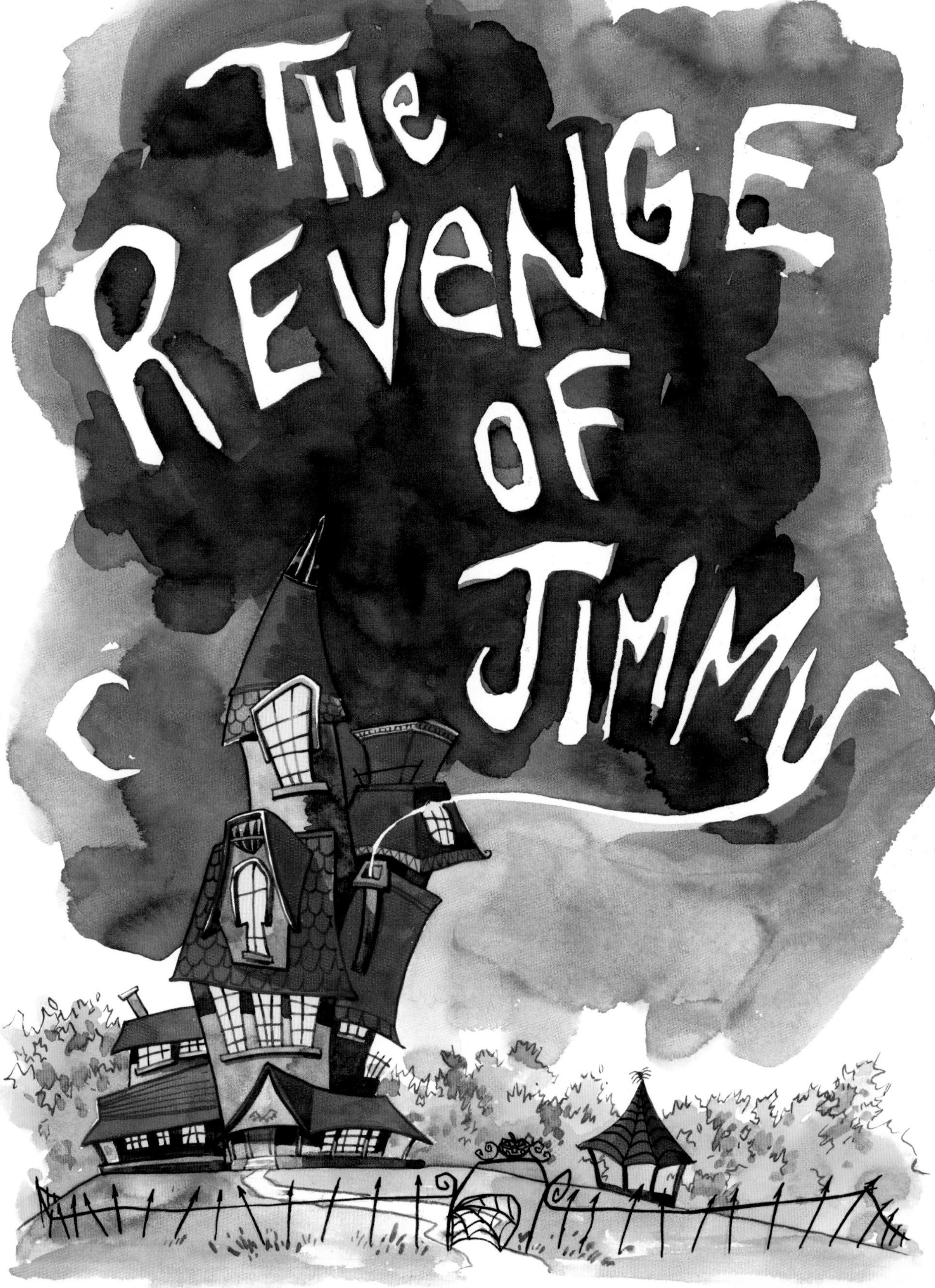
The Revenge of Jimmy

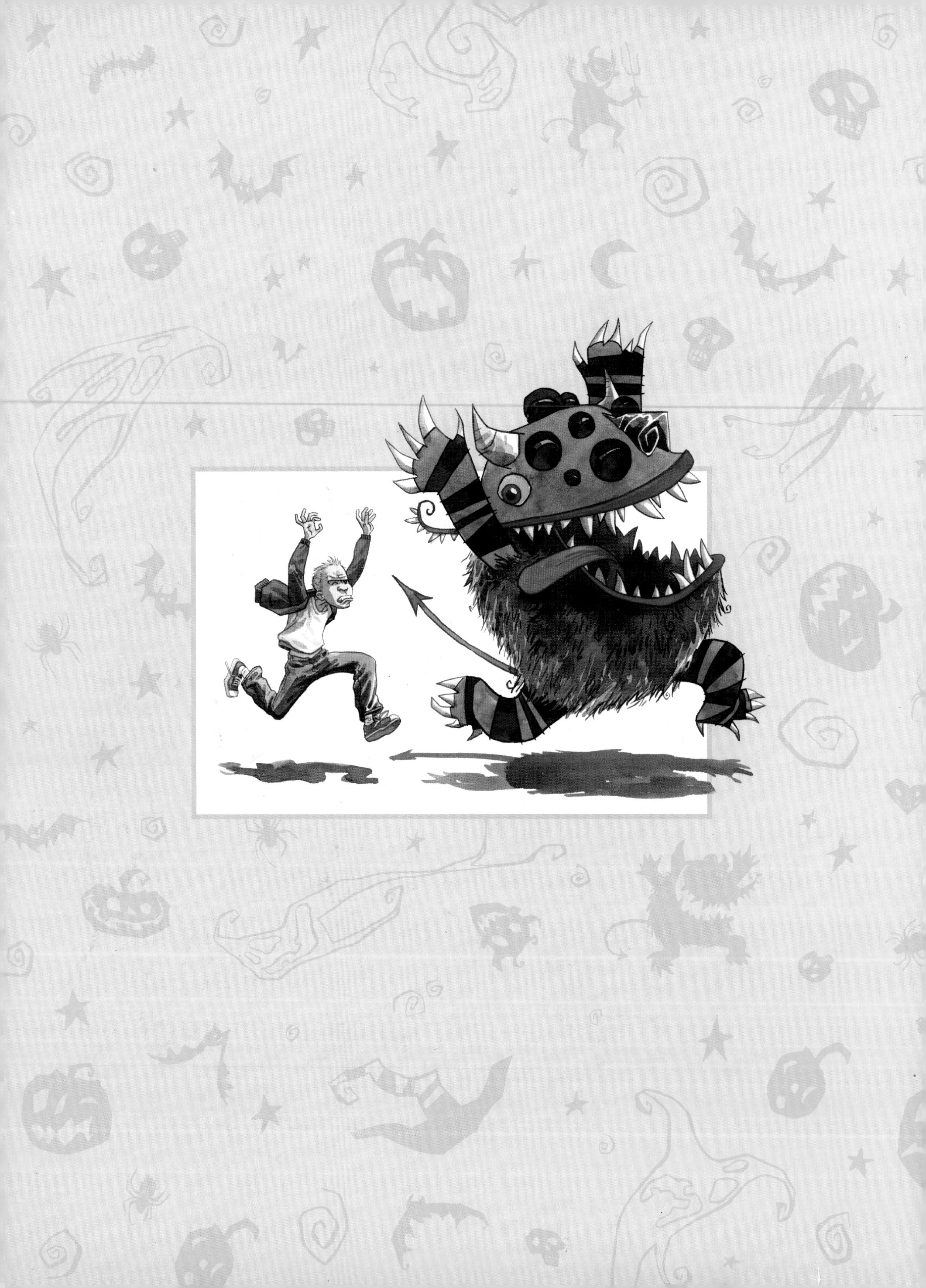

If there was one thing **Jimmy** knew about—it was **MONSTERS**! He had quivered with fear each day after school since the month of October began!

You see, monsters are free to roam the world each and every Halloween.
They lurk in the shadows waiting to gobble up the **tastiest** of snacks—
mischievous boys and girls—and Jimmy was sure they would be **coming to get him**.

Last Halloween, Jimmy and his gang had **barely escaped** the clutches of a giant, toothy horror! But the monster had a taste for him now, and in a matter of days it would be back—**under every** staircase and **behind every** door!

Since then, Jimmy had taken every precaution to prevent monsters from getting to him!
He **slept** with the lights on . . .

He kept a good supply of **flashlights** on hand at all times (monsters hate light) . . .

He made sure there was **no room** under his bed for monsters . . .

He **cleaned** out his closet . . .

And he never, ever, **EVER** went into the basement!

But on Halloween, monsters could go **wherever** they wanted! Clearly, he was doomed. Rules were rules! Jimmy thought and thought until his head was sore!

Hearing his parents gave Jimmy an **idea**!

A **nasty**, **mean**, **selfish**, and **devilish** idea!

On the other side of town, Jimmy's little cousin **Hannah Marie** couldn't wait for Halloween!

She **used to be** afraid of the dark and the things that went bump in the night, but she had a **Scary Godmother** who knew all about spooky things and shared her spectral secrets with the little girl! Hannah's fears poofed away and Halloween became her **favorite** holiday!

Hannah told Betty, her dog, all about the **first-ever** Halloween parade! Fantastic floats would flutter down the middle of town, leading costumed kids to the giant bonfire at the field house! There, they'd crown the kid whose costume was the best of all!

The **monster under the bed** grumbled out a gruff reply . . .

"Over on the Fright Side, we're **always** gettin' ready for Halloween—
it's what we're all about! But you know how crazy stuff gets at the **last minute**!
You should see the **commotion** goin' on at the Scary Godmother's house!

"She's cookin' up **potions** and bottling **frights**! Capturin' **shrieks** an' paintin'
clouds into the night! An' when every autumn leaf is crisped, and shivers chill
your bones—she gathers up the **Boozle**, 'cause their work has just begun!

"Her little bat wings lift her **high** into the sky, so she can better round up **rascals** for their favorite frightening night!

"Restless **souls** and **spirits** soar silently an' sigh, as giggling, ghoulish **ghosties** gang up as if to **fight**! Rousted by the Boozle, they take off in spectral flight!

"Through cobweb-coated corridors our spooky fairy flies! She'll wake the **undead King** and **Queen**, who slumber in their coffins and dream of **bloody** things.

"Once they are awakened, an **ice-cold mist** appears! It cushions vampire footsteps and allows them to draw near! In regal, nightmare velvet they float up the marble stair, with fantastic, flapping fanfare to join the **dark affair** . . .

"Creatures **bubble** from the ponds an' streams and **foam** out from the sea . . .

"While others grumble out from **under hills** and drop down from the trees . . .

"Leaving stragglers running far behind and **shouting**—"

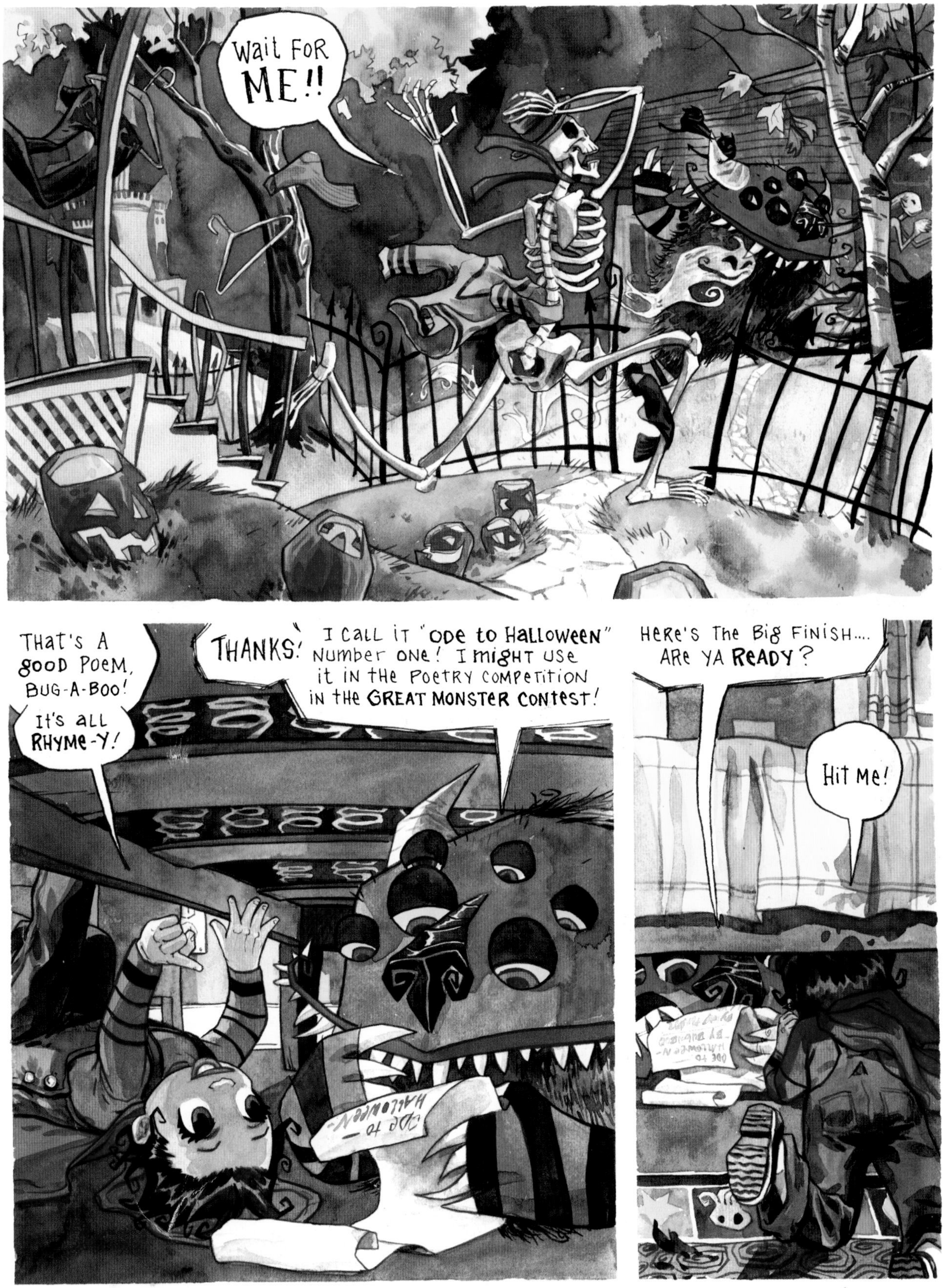

WAIT FOR ME!!
THAT'S A GOOD POEM, BUG-A-BOO!
IT'S ALL RHYME-Y!
THANKS! I CALL IT "ODE TO HALLOWEEN" NUMBER ONE! I MIGHT USE IT IN THE POETRY COMPETITION IN THE GREAT MONSTER CONTEST!
HERE'S THE BIG FINISH.... ARE YA READY?
HIT ME!

"Standing on a hilltop with the **moon** so **shiny bright** . . .

"Special **magic** words fly out like **bats** into the night!"

"A carved and stony bridge takes form an' stretches far an' wide . . .

"To carry nightmare creatures away from the Fright Side!

"So if you are out **Treatin'**, or playin' a **Trick** or two . . .
keep an eye peeled for a monster—they're out waiting for **YOU!**"

Bug-A-Boo's poem inspired Hannah at the dinner table.

Jimmy's mom was also inspired by Halloween—much to his dismay!

The next day, **everyone** discussed their plans for Halloween.
The whole school was crazy for it! **Except** Jimmy.

He spent his time formulating his elaborate anti-Halloween plot!

And when his parents thought he was snug in his bed,
Jimmy **crept** out into the deep, dark night to set his plan in motion!

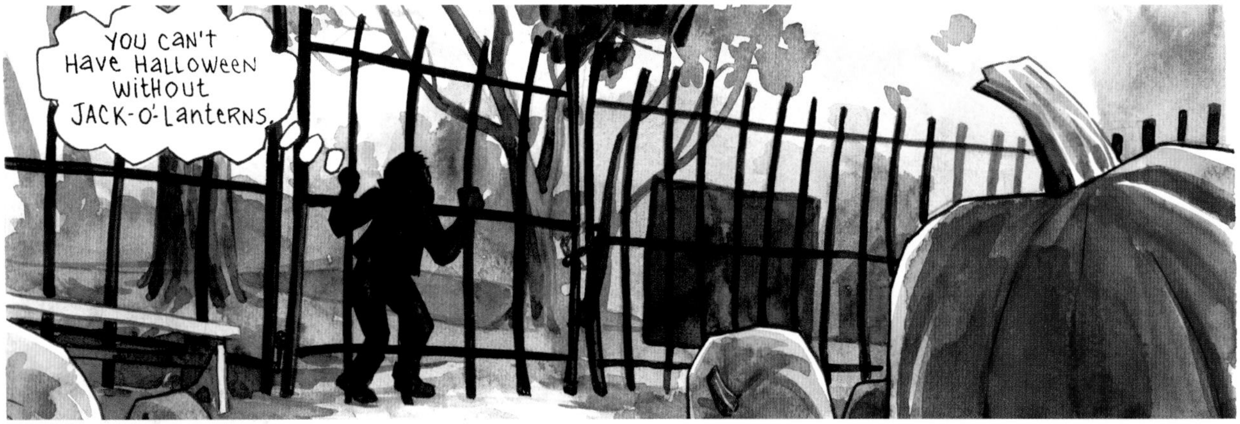
YOU CAN'T HAVE HALLOWEEN WITHOUT JACK-O'-LANTERNS.

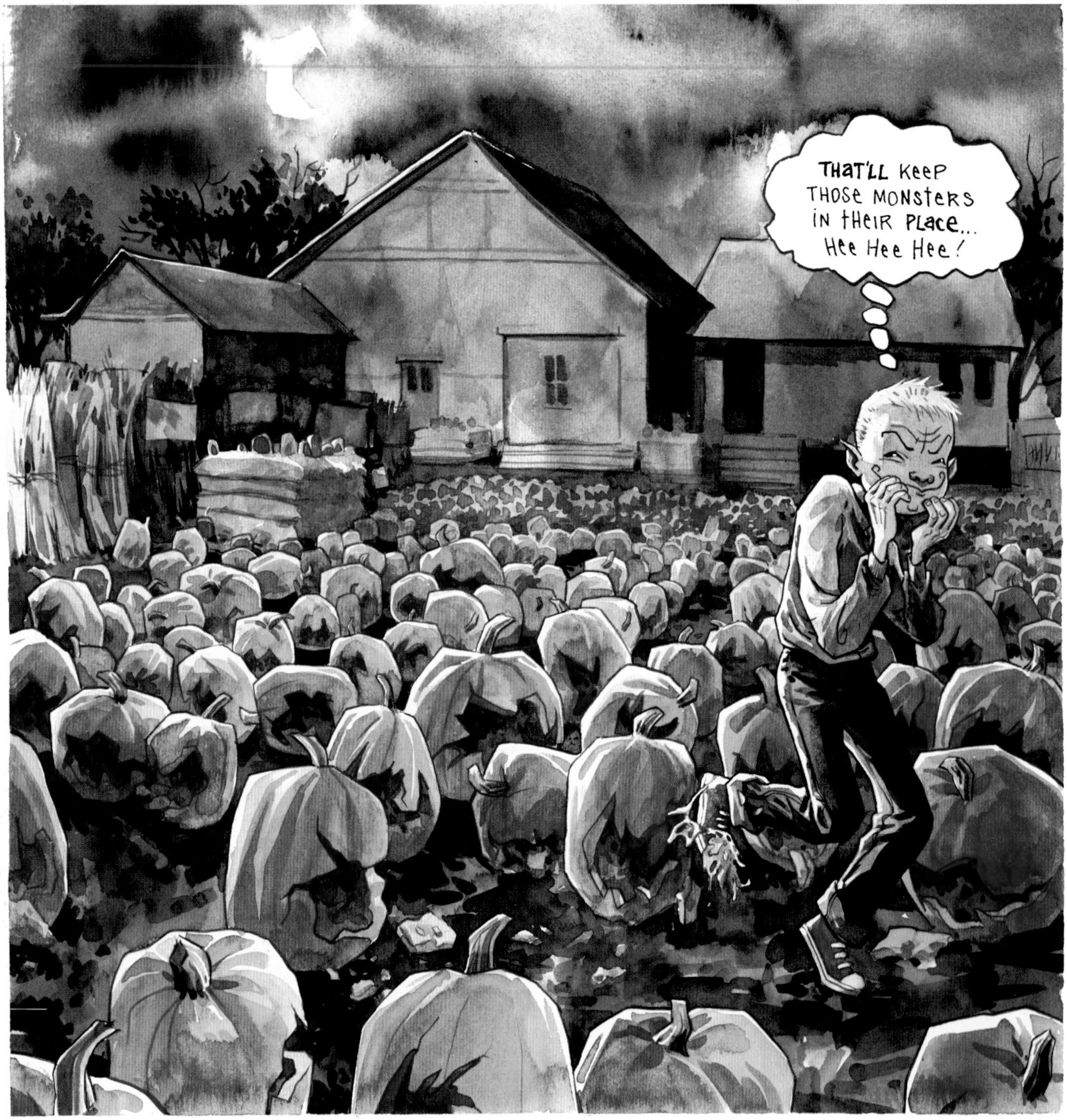
THAT'LL KEEP THOSE MONSTERS IN THEIR PLACE... HEE HEE HEE!

At that **exact** moment, a thick soup of **fog** poured all over the Fright Side!

And try as she might . . .

the Scary Godmother **couldn't** lead the way to the Halloween Bridge!

The next morning, when people came to buy their pumpkins, they found the pumpkin farm was **closed**! But why? Hannah rattled the gate until the farmer came over.

A cloud of disappointment settled over the crowd, and Jimmy felt triumphant . . .

. . . **until** little Emma spoke up!

The Anderson farm sold **all** of their pumpkins that day . . .

. . . and Jimmy sulked home to plan another dastardly deed!

The blanket of cold, clammy fog—**POOF**—disappeared,
and the bridge to Halloween was again free and clear!

Porches and windows sported toothsome new **jack-o'-lanterns** . . .

. . . that leered at Jimmy as he snuck back into the night!

The next afternoon, when people showed up to buy their Halloween costumes, they were greeted by Jimmy's nasty handiwork. **All** the costumes were **stamped** . . .

Jimmy's fingers clawed in the air while he danced with hunchbacked glee.

A **net** had stretched, silky and strong, across the Fright Side sky!
It hung over the trees and draped across the monsters' houses.

It **could not** be burned, or snipped, or broken . . .

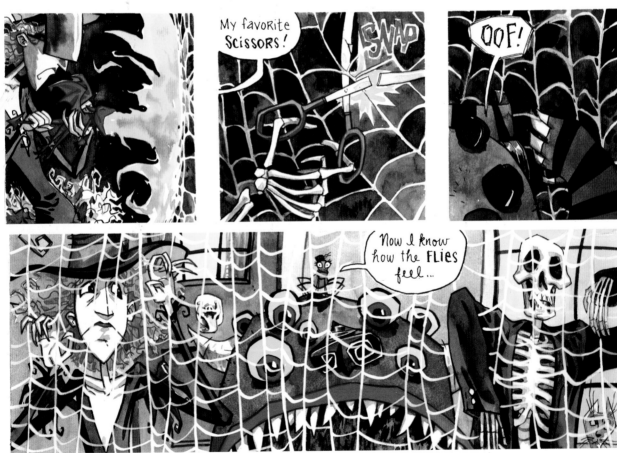

And it **trapped** them on the other side of Halloween!

Daryl and Bert got to talking . . .

And the weird web **withered** and was **whisked** away by the cinnamon wind!

Jimmy's nostrils snuffed up gulps of cool, autumn air as he passed houses bustling with costume creation! He **grumbled** at them on his way to commit mischief . . .

Jimmy could hardly contain his glee when everyone came
to the candy store to stock up for **Trick or Treats**.

The thought of Halloween **without candy** caused
a salty torrent to flow from the children's sad eyes.

Thunder rumbled in the inky clouds that hung in the Fright Side sky.
BOOM HOO HOO! The sky sobbed furiously—casting down sheets of stormy tears!

A raging river rushed through the hills and the valleys, rousting monsters out of their crypts
and caves. It swept them up the stairs to the tippy top of the Scary Godmother's house!

The flash flood fled as suddenly as it came, leaving the forests of the Fright Side decked out with **drippy-droppy** jewels!

Jimmy had **one night** left to stop Halloween from coming, but he'd already run through his list of monster-stopping tricks! What to do . . . What to do . . . ?

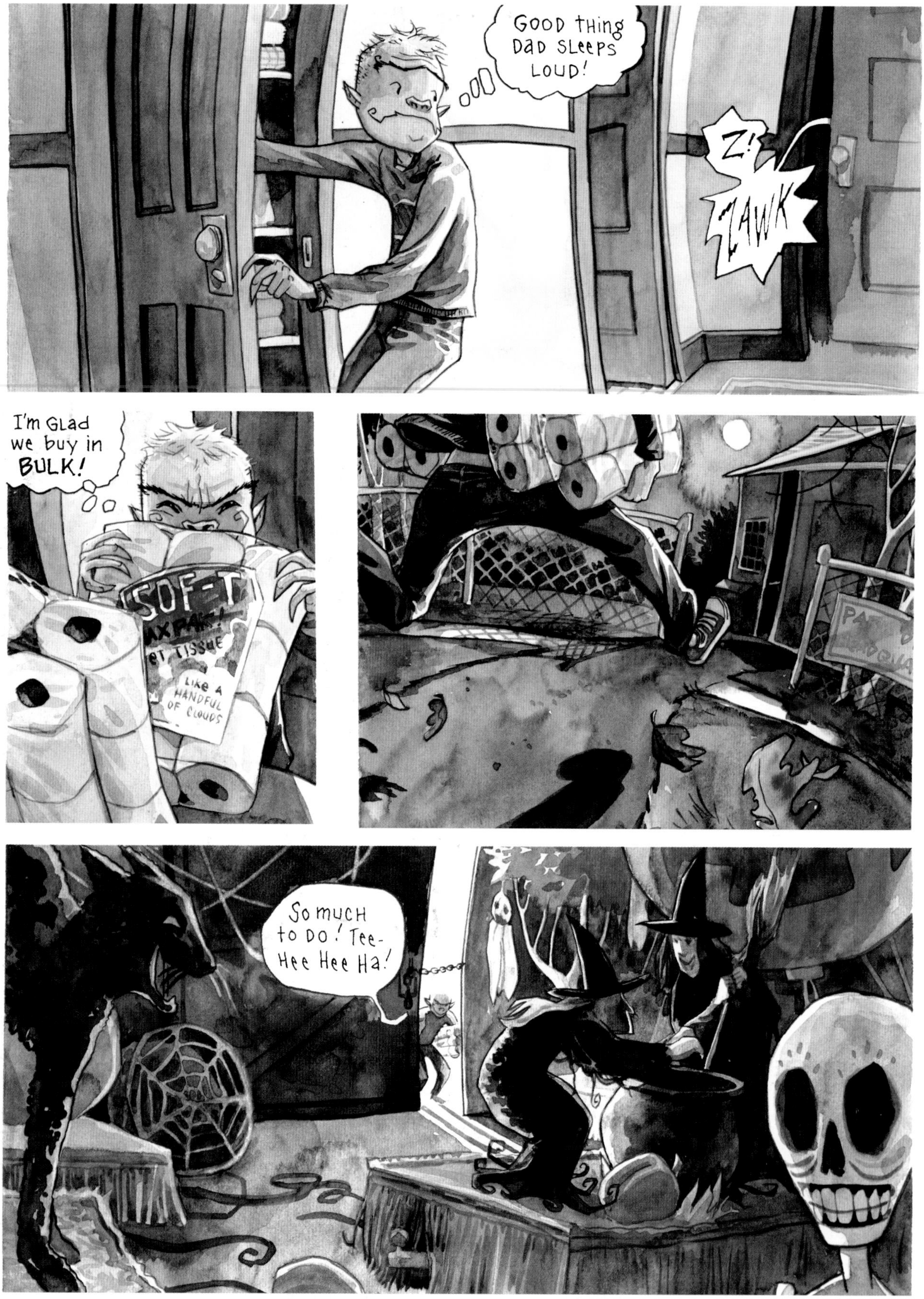

GOOD THING DAD SLEEPS LOUD!
Z! ZAWK
I'm Glad we buy in BULK!
SOF-T
LIKE A HANDFUL OF CLOUDS
So much to do! Tee-Hee Hee Ha!

He worked **all through** the night . . .

And was **back in his bed** by the time his mother came in to check on him!

It was **Halloween day**! Hip, hip, **HOORAY**! Brightly colored **leaves** scuttled past children dressed in **fine**, **homemade** costumes, **vainly competing** for some kind of attention! Ghoulish little girls and teeny, tiny terrors rushed past storybook mermaids and transistor robots—all **masquerading** their way to school!

Copious amounts of **cupcakes** were consumed in classroom parties.

And after school it was **ding-dong ditch** and **target practice** for every door!

Late Halloween afternoon, Jimmy crept out of his "sick" bed to see the heartache his handiwork had caused. He **spied** on the parade volunteers and gargled with glee!

Meanwhile, the monsters merrily made their way toward the Halloween Bridge decked out in their finest Nightmare Wear!

The main streets were **lined** with people who waited for a parade that would never arrive! Hannah waited and waited, until she could **wait no more!**

Betty pulled Hannah towards the field house, and the crowd soon followed along.

The children were the first to arrive.

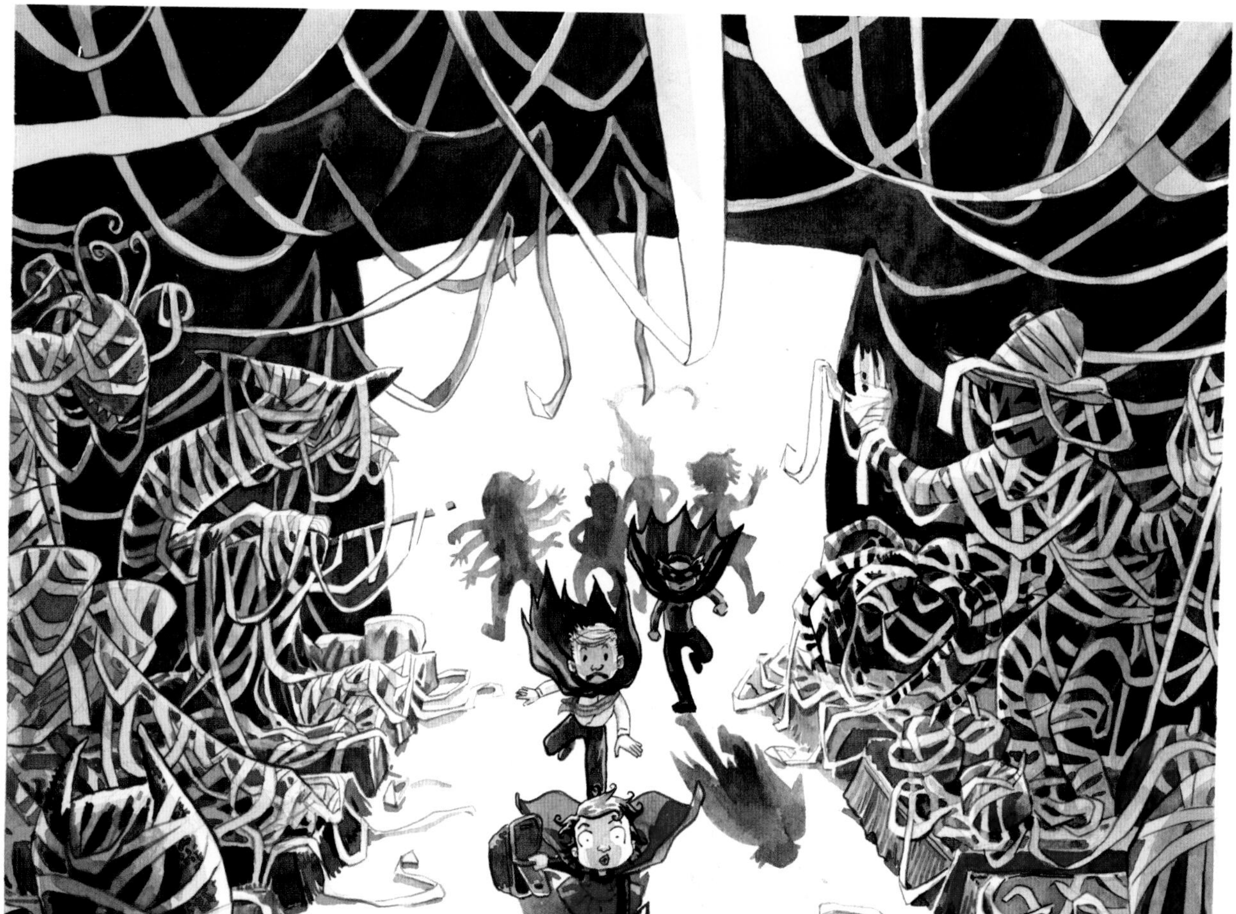

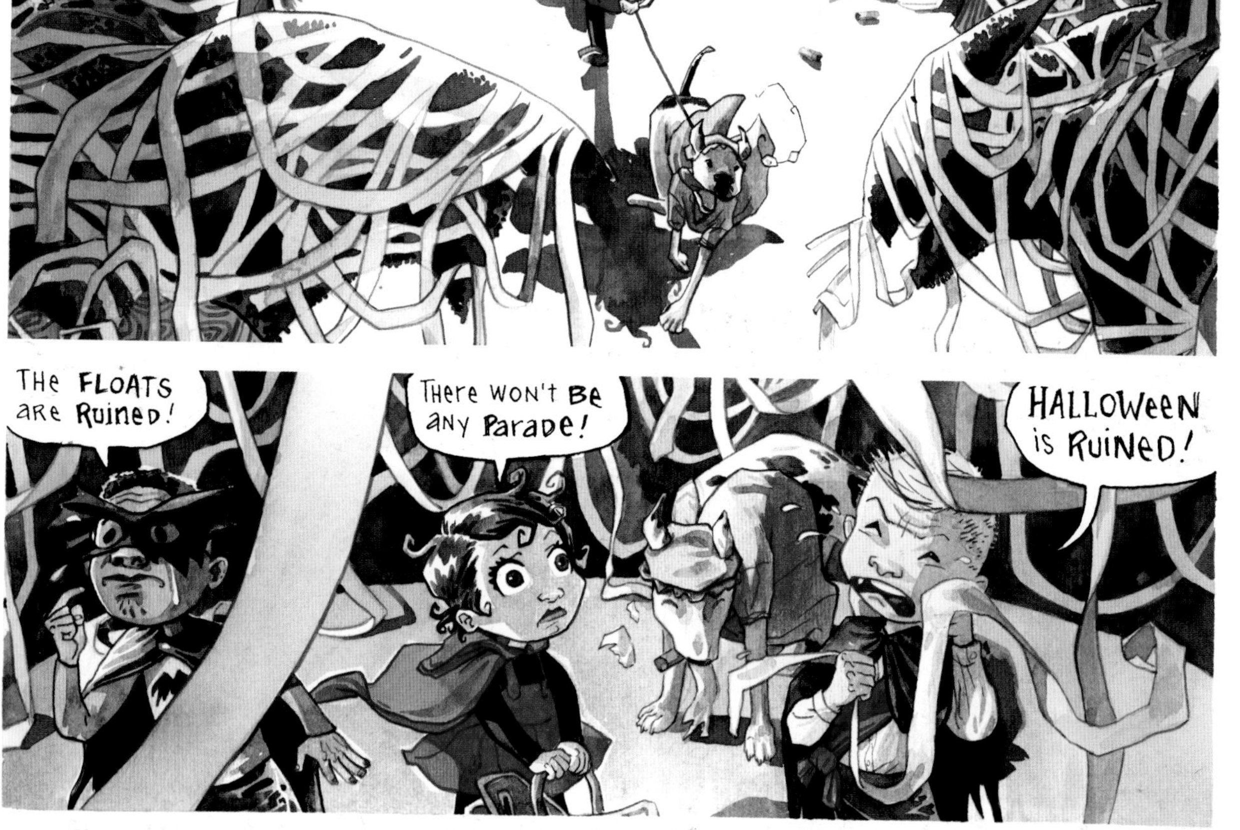
THE FLOATS are RUINED!
THERE WON'T BE any PARADE!
HALLOWEEN is RUINED!

Thick, varicose vines twiggled out of the earth and obscured the Halloween Bridge!
The intestinal innards reached way into the sky—
they even went higher than the Scary Godmother could fly!

A wild, warm wind whispered all around them, drying their salty tears!

The crowd "**oohed**" and "**aahed**" as Hannah explained.

And with **that**, the terrible tower of thorns toppled and Halloween **busted out** all over!
A cavalcade of creatures flew high with kids and floats in tow!
Real ghosts glided overhead in an ectoplasmic show!

Mister Pettibone clacked and the monsters **mashed** to the light of a magical fire!

Jimmy **puffed up** with pride, like a marshmallow in the microwave!
He clawed his way into the clearing and **belted** out in a baritone bark—

Jimmy had become **so horrible**, he **scared** even **Bug-A-Boo!**

Jimmy pulled with all of his might, but he wasn't heavy enough to weigh down the balloon!

And the monsters he had feared **did not** gobble him up.
They **helped** him to **save** the Halloween his deeds made . . .

Safe on the ground, Jimmy glowed with **gratitude**.

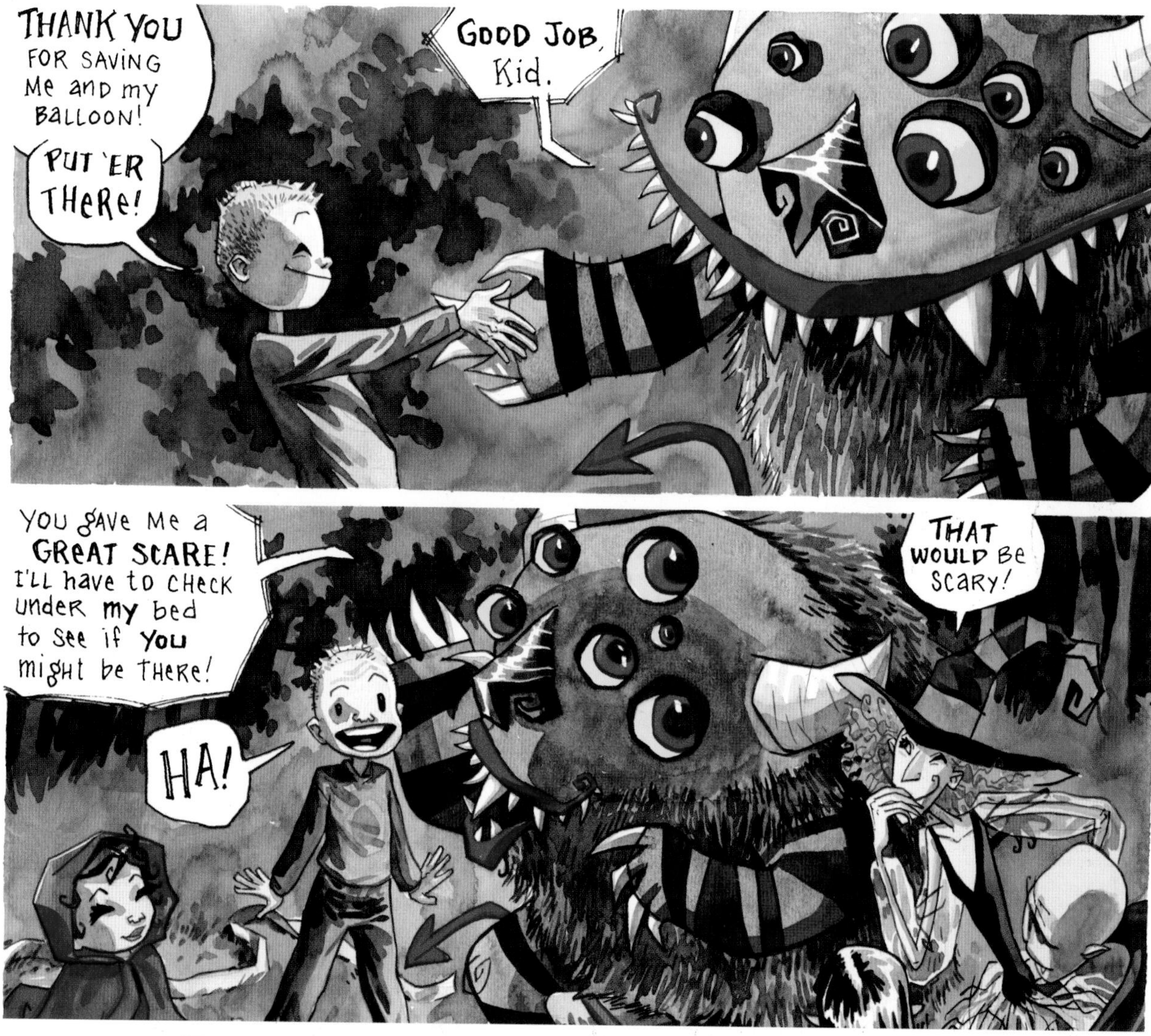
THANK YOU FOR SAVING Me and my BALLOON!
PUT 'ER THeRe!
GOOD JOB, Kid.
YOU gAVe Me a GReAT SCARE! I'LL have to CHeck under my bed to See if YOU might be THeRe!
HA!
THAT WOULD Be ScARY!

When **costumes** were judged—Jimmy was awarded **First Prize**!

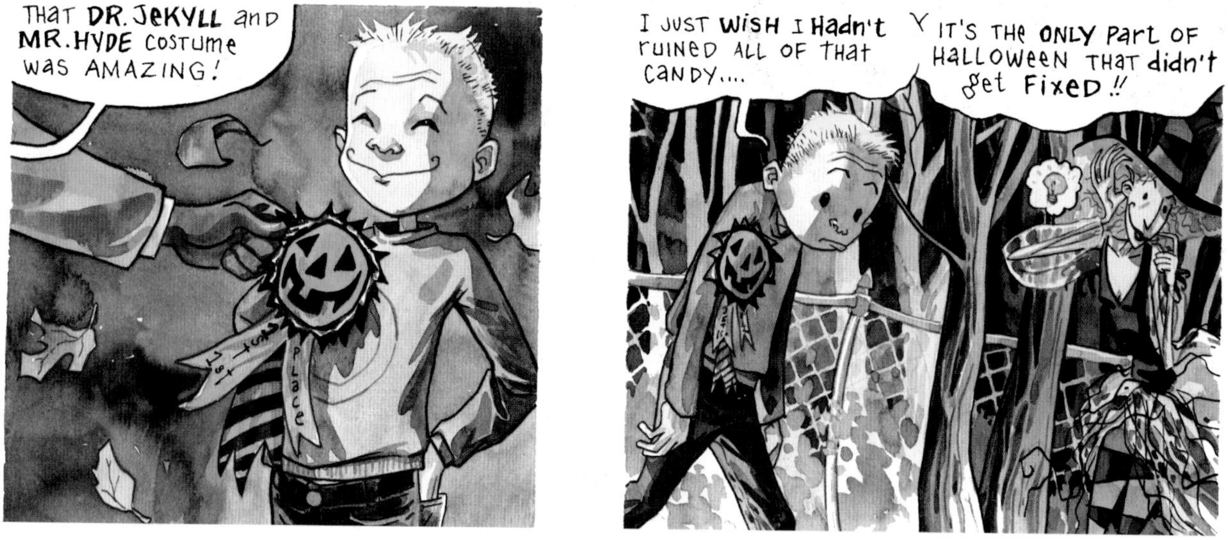
THAT DR. JeKYLL and MR. HYDE COSTUme WAS AMAZING!
I JUST WISH I Hadn't ruIneD ALL OF THat CANDY....
IT'S THe ONLY Part OF HaLLOWeeN THAT didn't get FIXeD!!

Haunting, soft music blew out of the trees!
Jimmy ran **lickety-split**, so he was the first one to see the magical sight!

There were enough **treats** for **everyone** with plenty left over! All the folks agreed, it was the best **Halloween** that they could remember! And for Jimmy, **revenge** certainly was **sweet**!

THE END

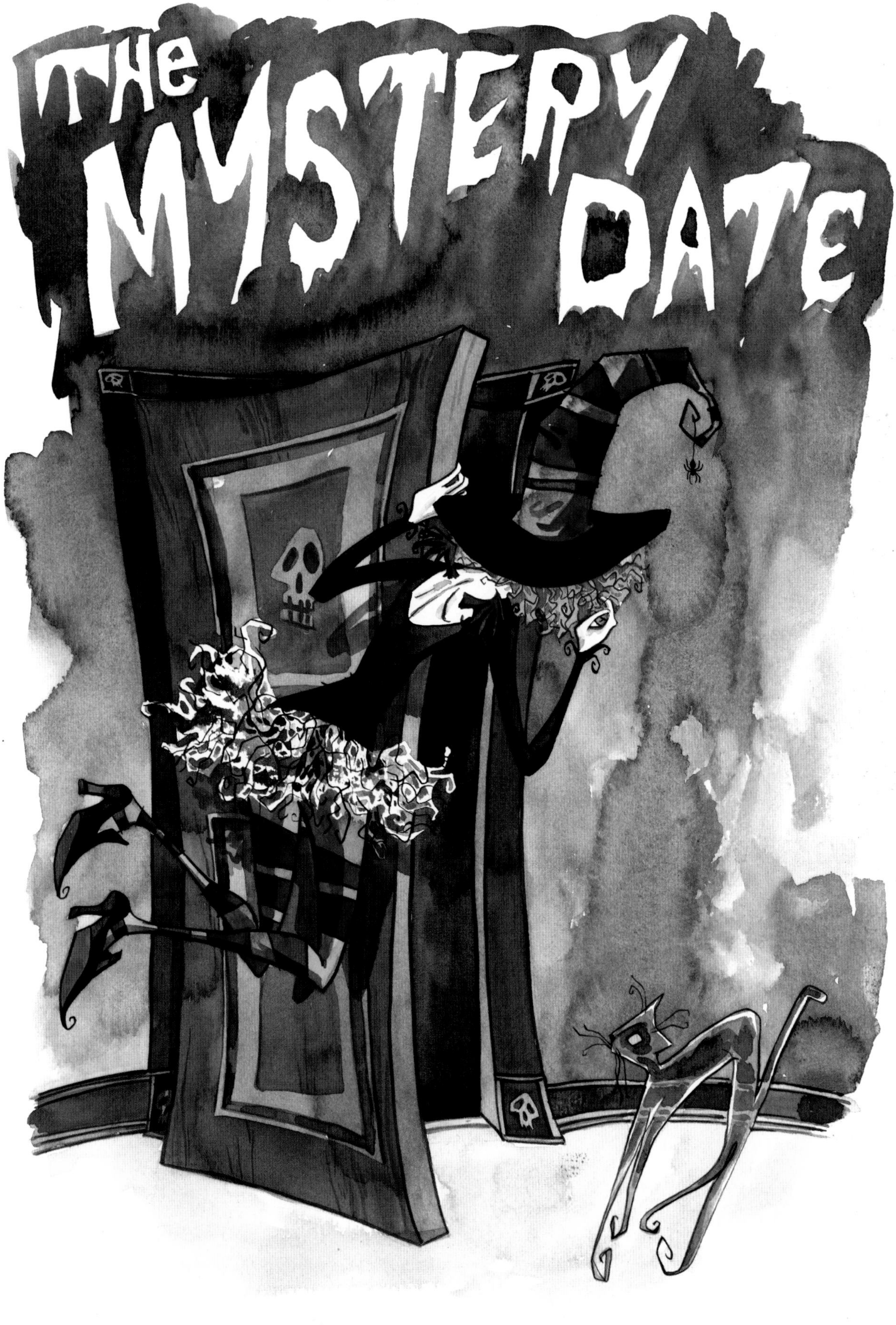
THE MYSTERY DATE

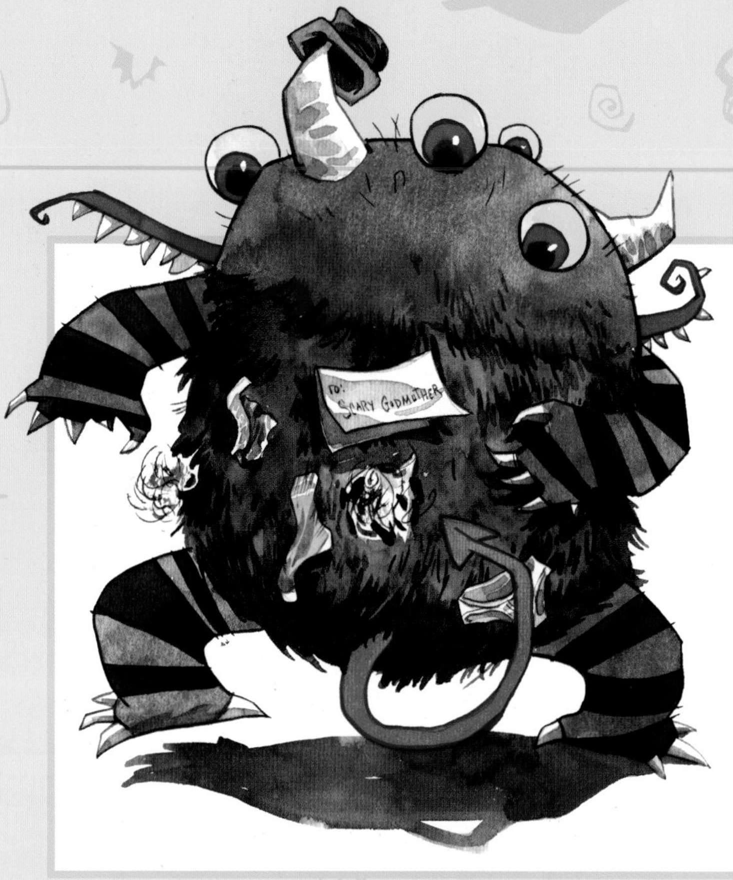
TO: SCARY GODMOTHER

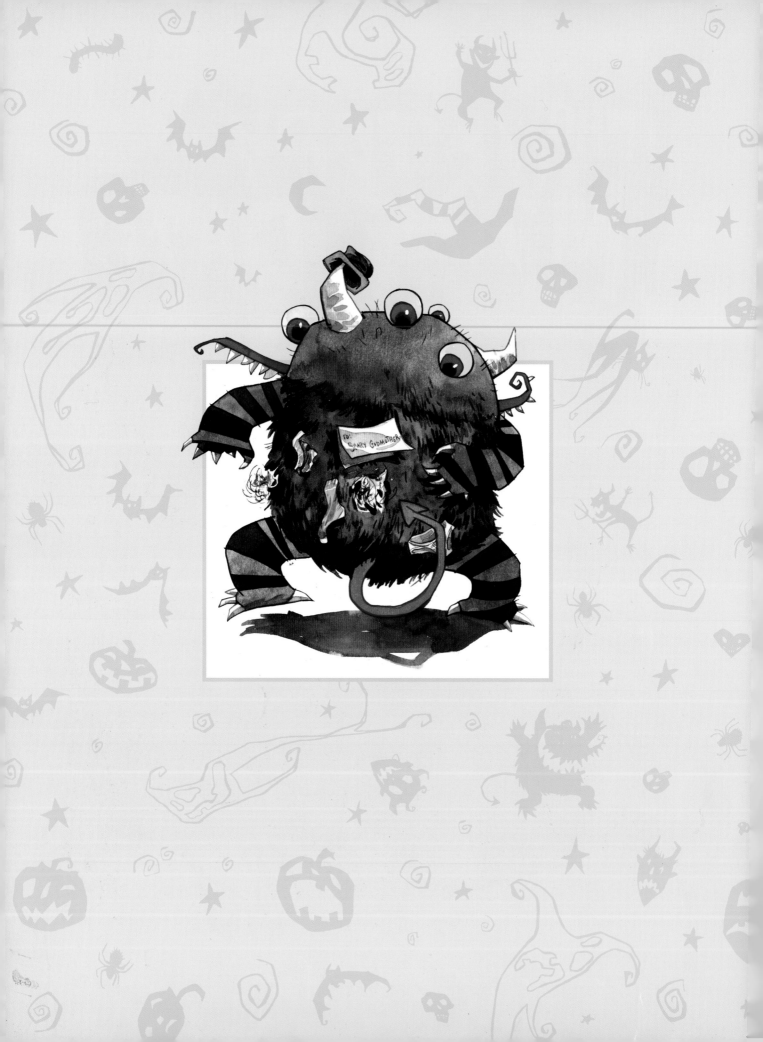

uried alive! With every turn the car made, Hannah Marie was covered in candy corns, pummeled by pumpkins, and battered by bats. As her mom pulled the car into the driveway, Hannah hollered . . .

If Hannah survived the ride home, she could help her mom with the party plans.

You see, her parents were hosting a Halloween party so big, that the entire neighborhood could come. The block would be closed to traffic so there could be games and dancing in the street! Everyone would decorate their houses and make treats to share. Hannah's mom was in charge of the planning and she checked her guest list to make sure she hadn't forgotten anyone.

Hannah rushed to her room, to make invitations for all of the Monsters she knew.

So, at bedtime, when all of the other kids in town did
their best to avoid the Monster under the Bed . . .

. . . Hannah addressed him by name . . .

. . . and the Monster under the Bed grumbled back at her.

Visiting the place where the Monsters dwell can be a rather tricky procedure,
unless, of course, you're friends with a monster or two like little Hannah is.
She followed the secret steps as Bug-A-Boo looked on. This is what she did . . .

The Fright Side is the spooky place where Hannah's Scary Godmother lives.
She shares her house with Boozle, her ghostie; Mister Pettibone, the Skeleton
in the Closet; and Bug-A-Boo, the Monster under the Bed. They are always
doing Halloween things, and Hannah can visit them whenever she likes.

Hannah helped move sinister squash outside to the Scary Godmother's porch. Mister Pettibone was quick as a flash, and with only one match, he'd lit up all the jagged-edged faces!

Pulling the pile of party invitations from her pajamas, Hannah asked each of her pals to attend. The creatures roared with dark delight at the prospect of a party.

With Hannah strapped on to her comfy-seat broom, the Scary Godmother flew nearly as high as the moon. Why? To deliver those invitations Fright Side style, of course—by Scare Mail!

The vampires who lived next door to the Scary Godmother accepted . . .

. . . as did the Werewolf in the forest (and his mom).

The patrons of the local watering hole were eager to attend.

During lunch, the kids grew excited as the plans for the party progressed. Hannah's cousin Jimmy listened as they bragged to each other.

There was much to do at the Scary Godmother's house before All Hallow's Eve: scattering spider webbing, squeaking every door, releasing vintage spirits, toasting treats, and more. Hannah always lent a helping hand. Amidst the autumn activity, Bug-A-Boo almost went unnoticed, which is hard to do when you're a big, blue Monster!

It was Orson, the Vampire boy, who first noticed the mysterious letter.

The Scary Godmother plucked the paper from Bug-A-Boo's prickly fur and read it.

Mister Pettibone popped out of the closet with an answer.

Bug-A-Boo crunched out a crispy explanation (complete with crumbs) . . .

. . . which Mister Pettibone promptly corrected.

Hannah and Orson thought about the Secret Admirer: who could it be?
They hatched a plan to identify the monstery mystery man.

When no one was looking, they sneaked out the door into the Fright Side Night.

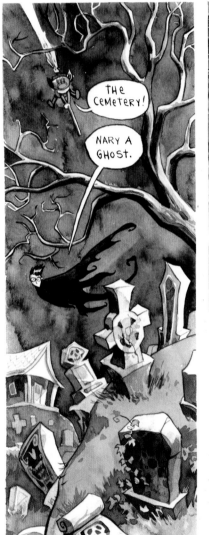

The tiny detectives looked far and wide, searching every haunted hangout
on the Fright Side. Just when they thought their luck had run out,
they came upon something that caused them to shout . . .

The Monster Truck Rally was a frightful phantom fest. Monster men brought their mean machines and put them to the test. Surely the Scary Godmother's secret admirer was in this creepy crowd. Dastardly devils, enthusiastic ectoplasm, rambunctious revenants, wild werewolves—you name it, and it was there!

Like flies at a picnic, they flitted around, dropping choice tidbits: gossip unbound! A little whisper here, and a bit of stretched truth there . . . and they set their plan in motion.

Sure they were fibs, but a few harmless little
white lies wouldn't cause any trouble—would they?

As they took to the skies, the conspirators congratulated themselves on a job quite well done . . .

. . . unaware of just what their work had begun . . .

. . . unaware of how Monsters love competition for fun!

And as quick as a flash, once the word got around . . .
eligible Monsters shambled their way across town!

With moans, groans, and grumbles, in groups of two, three, and four . . .
they made their way up to the Scary Godmother's door.

They camped out on her doorstep . . .

. . . cooked her nine breakfast treats.

They lay down in some puddles . . .

. . . to keep mud off her feets.

They made monster music . . .

. . . to serenade her at night.

They trampled her garden with their wrestling fights!

While watching TV . . .

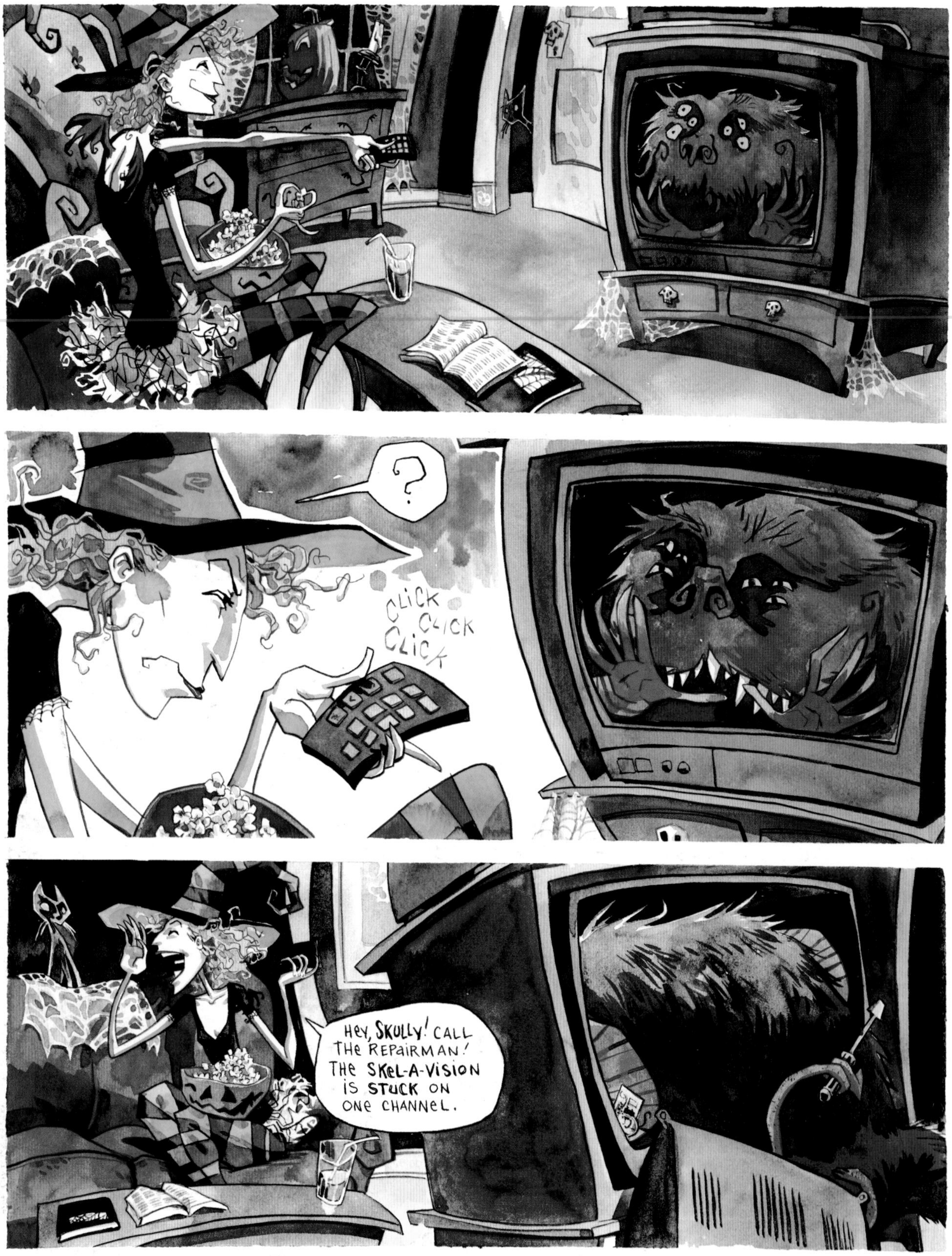
?
CLICK CLICK CLICK
HEY, SKULLY! CALL THE REPAIRMAN! THE SKEL-A-VISION IS STUCK ON ONE CHANNEL.

. . . or taking a bath . . .

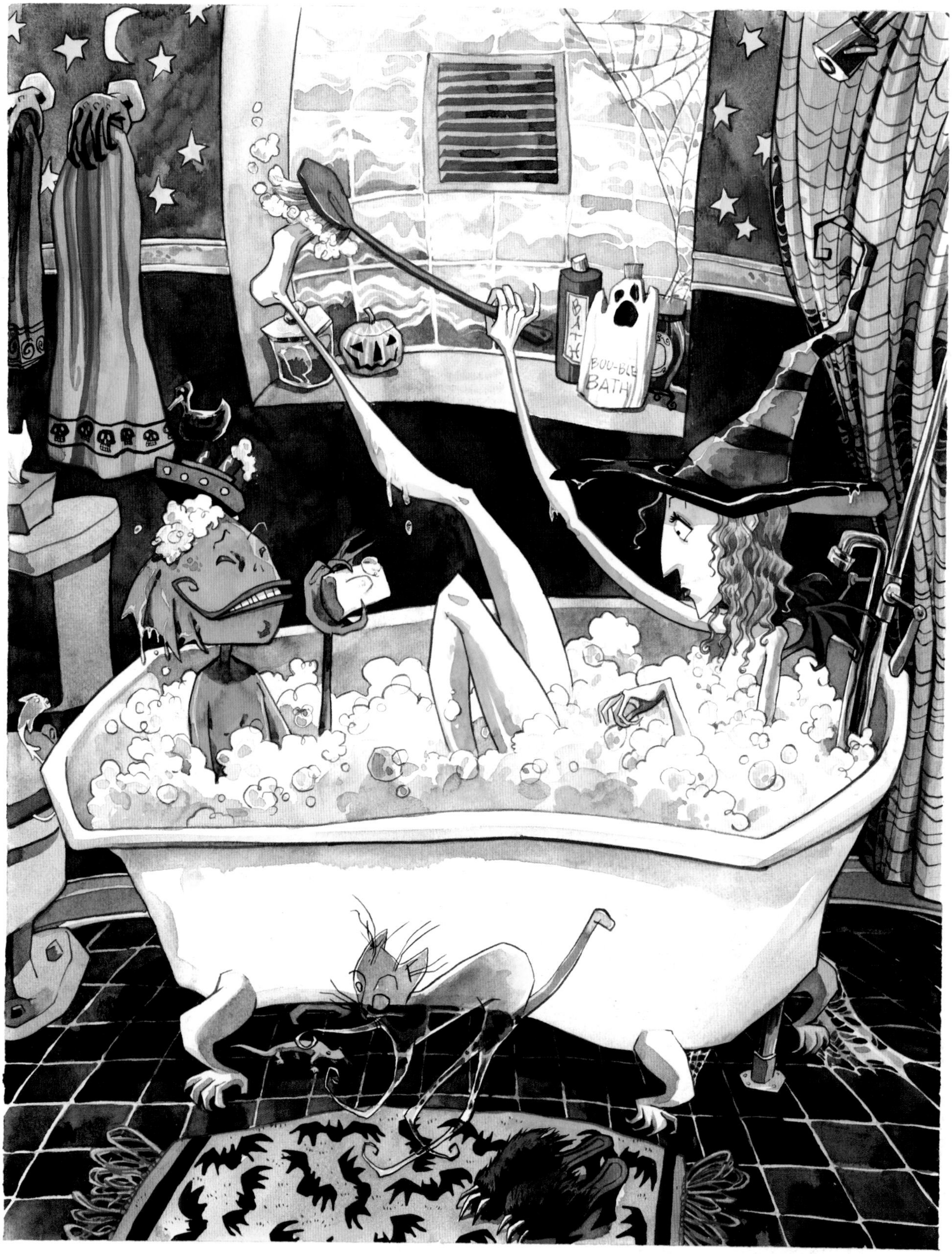
BATH
BOO-BLE BATH

. . . Monsters popped up in Scary Godmother's path.

And on her way home from the gross-ery store . . .

. . . the confused little spookstress could take it no more!

The Scary Godmother frantically huffed and puffed her way back home.

Skully Pettibone, the Skeleton in the Closet, was the keeper of all secrets.
He popped out of the armoire to clarify the situation.

Hannah and Orson fessed up as Bug-A-Boo came home.

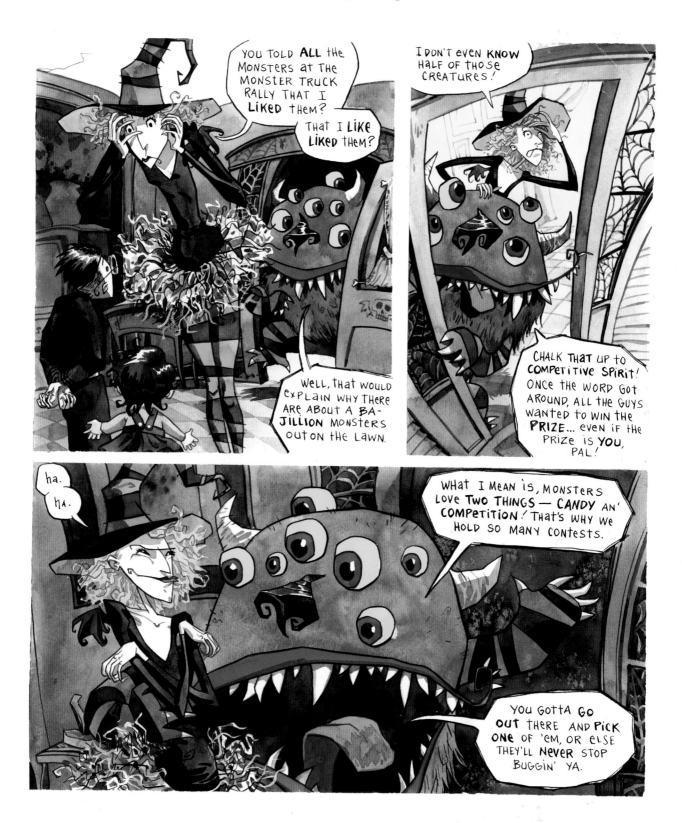

And so, the Scary Godmother . . . ventured . . . outside to set things straight.

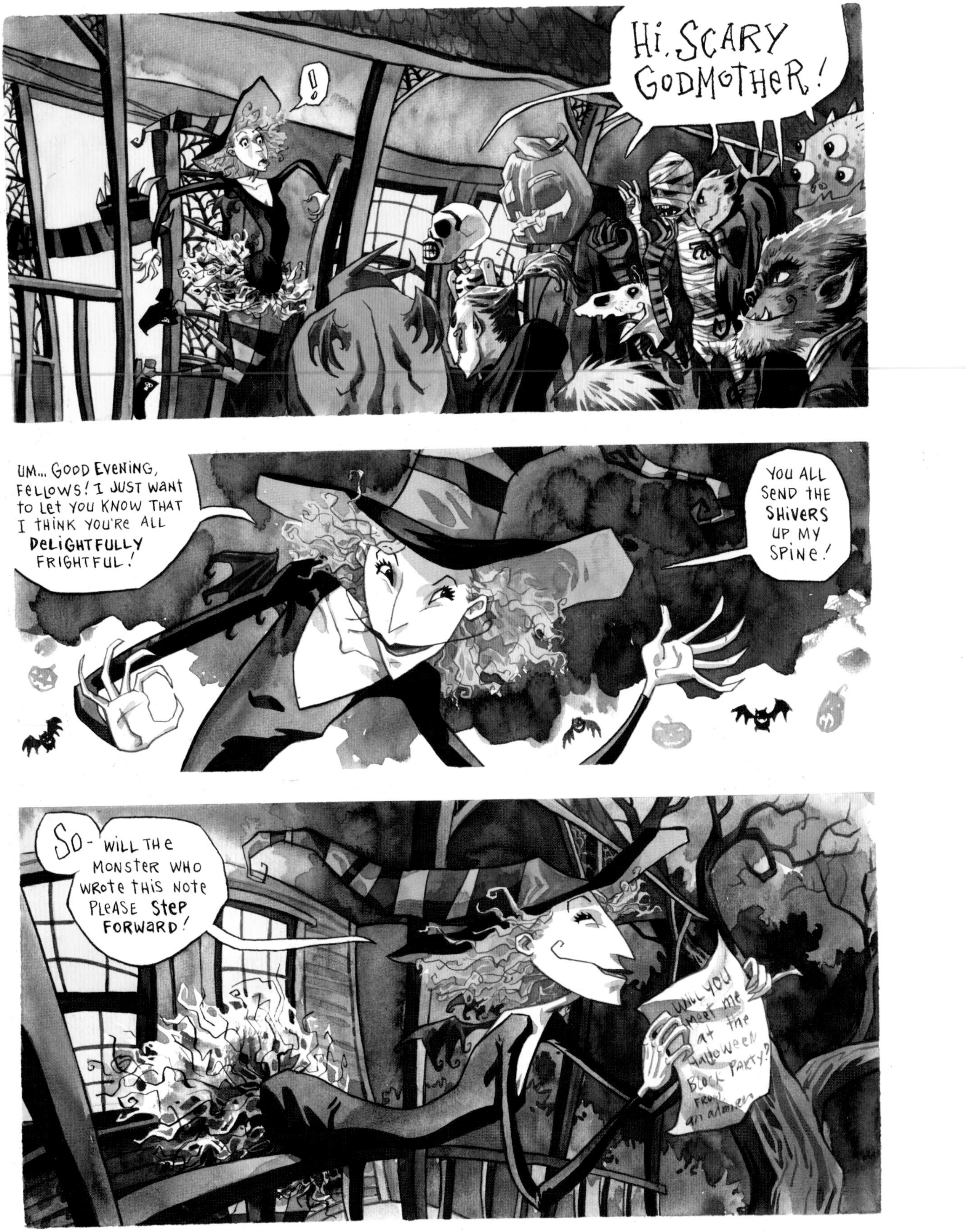
!
Hi, SCARY GODMOTHER!
UM... GOOD EVENING, FELLOWS! I JUST WANT TO LET YOU KNOW THAT I THINK YOU'RE ALL DELIGHTFULLY FRIGHTFUL!
YOU ALL SEND THE SHIVERS UP MY SPINE!
SO- WILL THE MONSTER WHO WROTE THIS NOTE PLEASE STEP FORWARD!
Will you meet me at the Halloween Block Party?
From an admirer

From nightmare to ghoul, the paper was passed around.

Amongst all of these monsters, the author was not found!

"Not me! Not me!" each monster explained as they took
to the air or shambled back to coffins and caves.

The Scary Godmother exclaimed once they were out of sight . . .

On Halloween day, Hannah's street was blocked off, so cars could not drive down it.
Each family brought their treats and decorations to the sidewalk and by nightfall,
the haunted carnival was complete.

Hannah slipped on her costume and ran out, lickety-split, to join the fun.

And what did our Scary Godmother do? Well, she got all gussied up!

From her head . . .

. . . to her toes.

She dressed in her most witchified Hallow's Eve clothes!
(With all of the necessary accessor-aries . . .)

. . . they chased children with glee!

While the Scary Godmother stood waiting under a tree.

She waited . . .

. . . and waited . . .

. . . and waited.

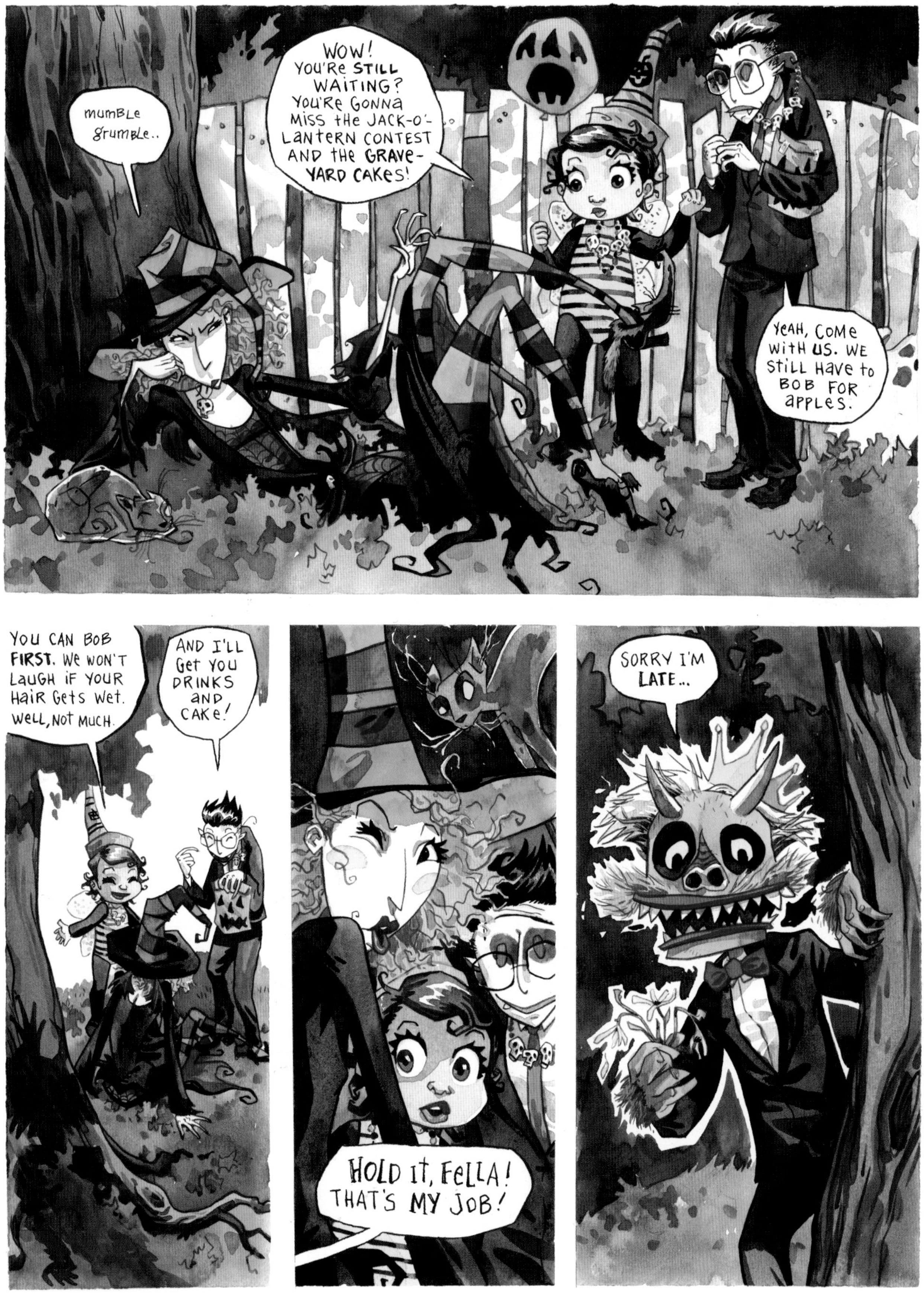

mumble grumble..
WOW! You're STILL WAITING? You're Gonna miss the JACK-o'-Lantern CONTEST AND the GRAVE-YARD CAKES!
Yeah, Come with US. We still have to BOB FOR apples.
You CAN BOB FIRST. We WON'T Laugh if YOUR Hair Gets Wet. WELL, NOT MUCH.
AND I'LL Get you DRINKS and CAKE!
HOLD it, FeLLA! THAT'S MY JOB!
SORRY I'M LATE...

It was Jimmy who stepped up to escort the Scary Godmother to the festivities!
He had said that he'd bring something none of the other kids would guess . . .
and boy, was he right! He brought a date!

Anyone could say they'd brought a favorite cake or treat to a party . . .
but how many could claim to have brought the Queen of Halloween?

So the King of the Monsters and his Halloween Queen enjoyed their All Hallow's evening.

Refreshments were in order after all of that fun,
so the creepy couple crept over to the table of treats.

But when they got there . . .

THE END

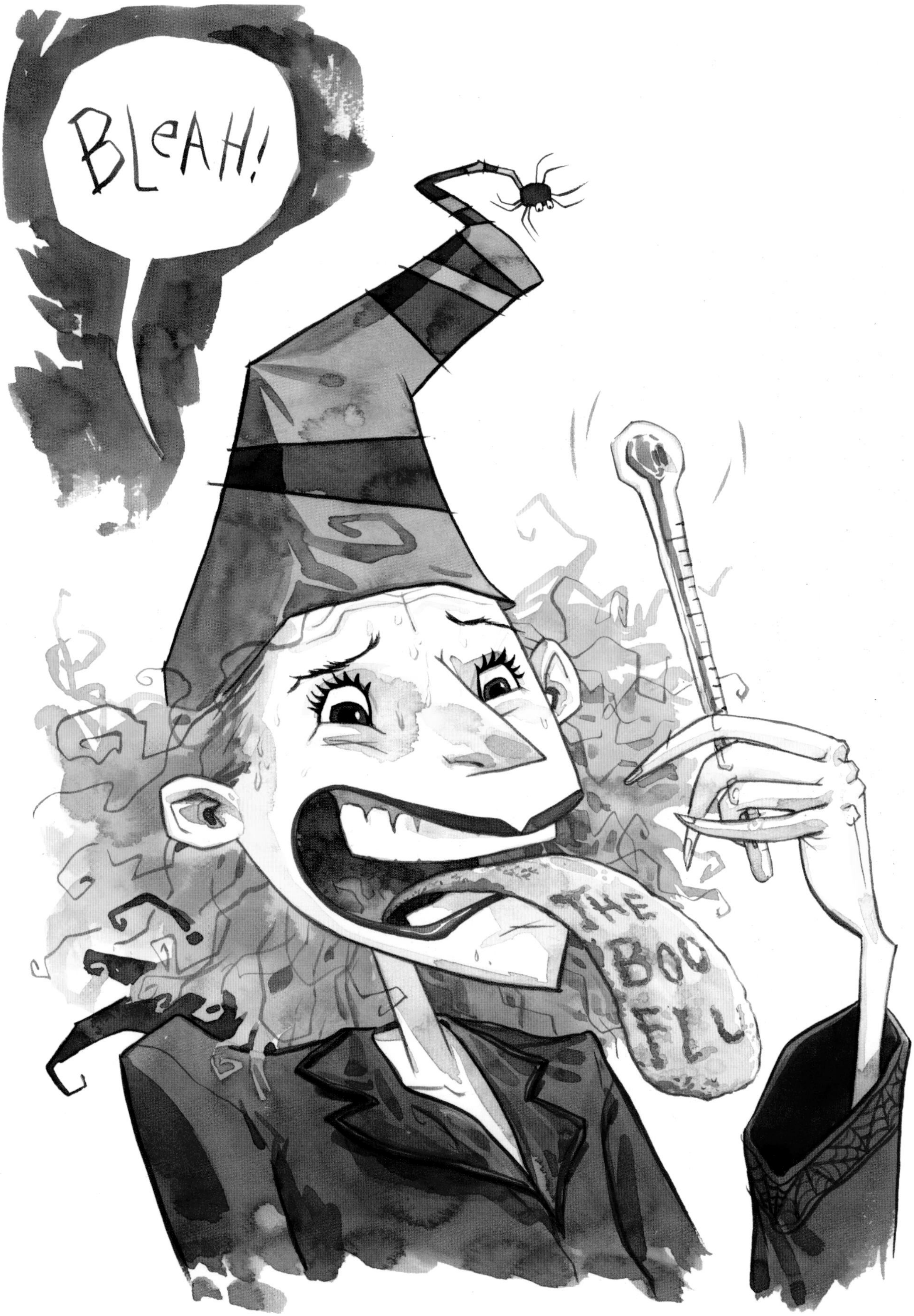
BLeAH!
THE BOO FLU

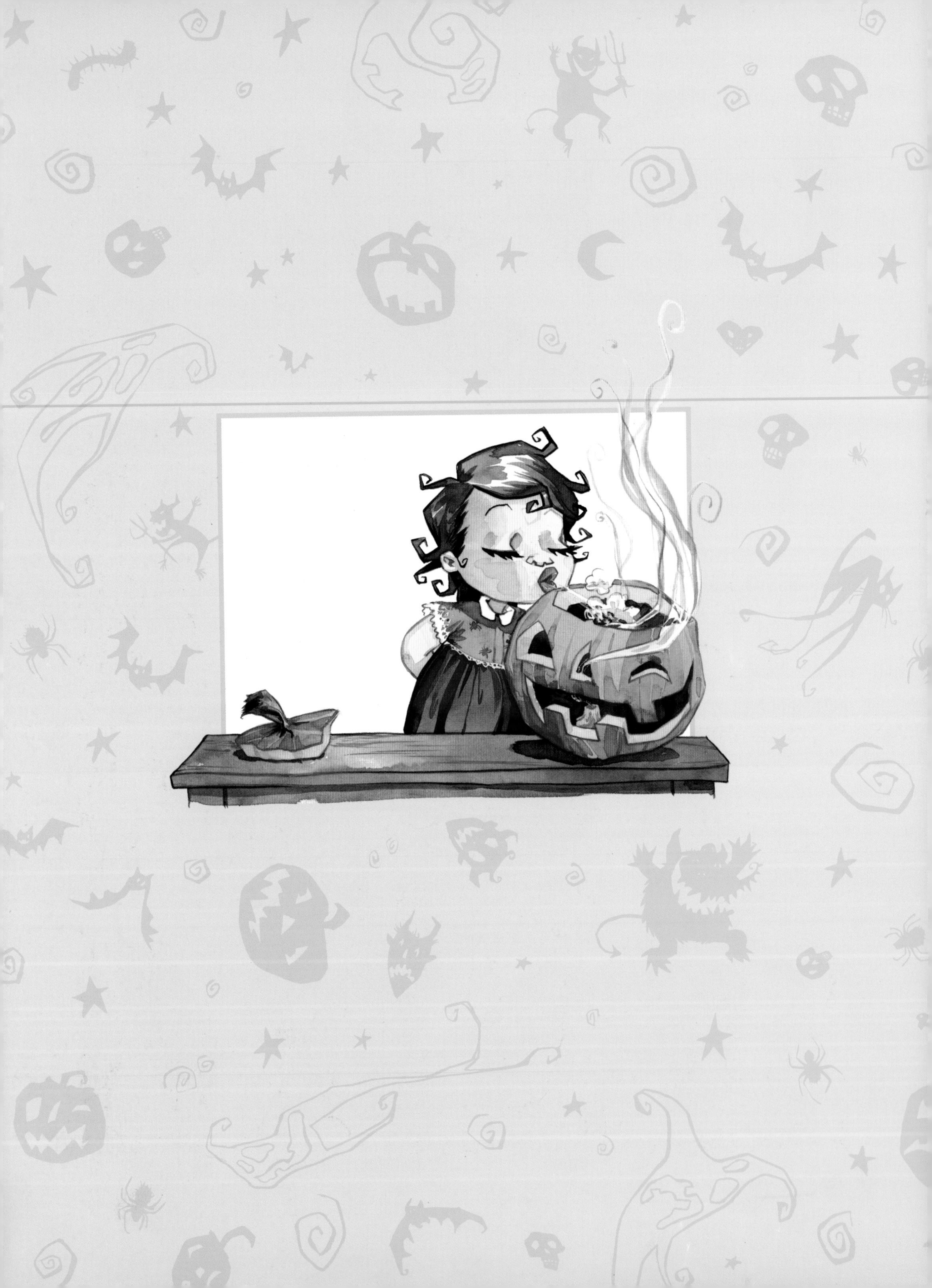

On a dark autumn night with lots of work left to do, the Scary Godmother contracted the dreaded Boo Flu!

First came the sweats, then her face got the pox.

She shivered and shook from her head to her socks.

While she sneezed and she coughed, her friends put her
to bed, and a weak little voice whispered out of her head.

The monsters all fretted and ran willy-nilly. Hannah giggled because she thought they looked silly.

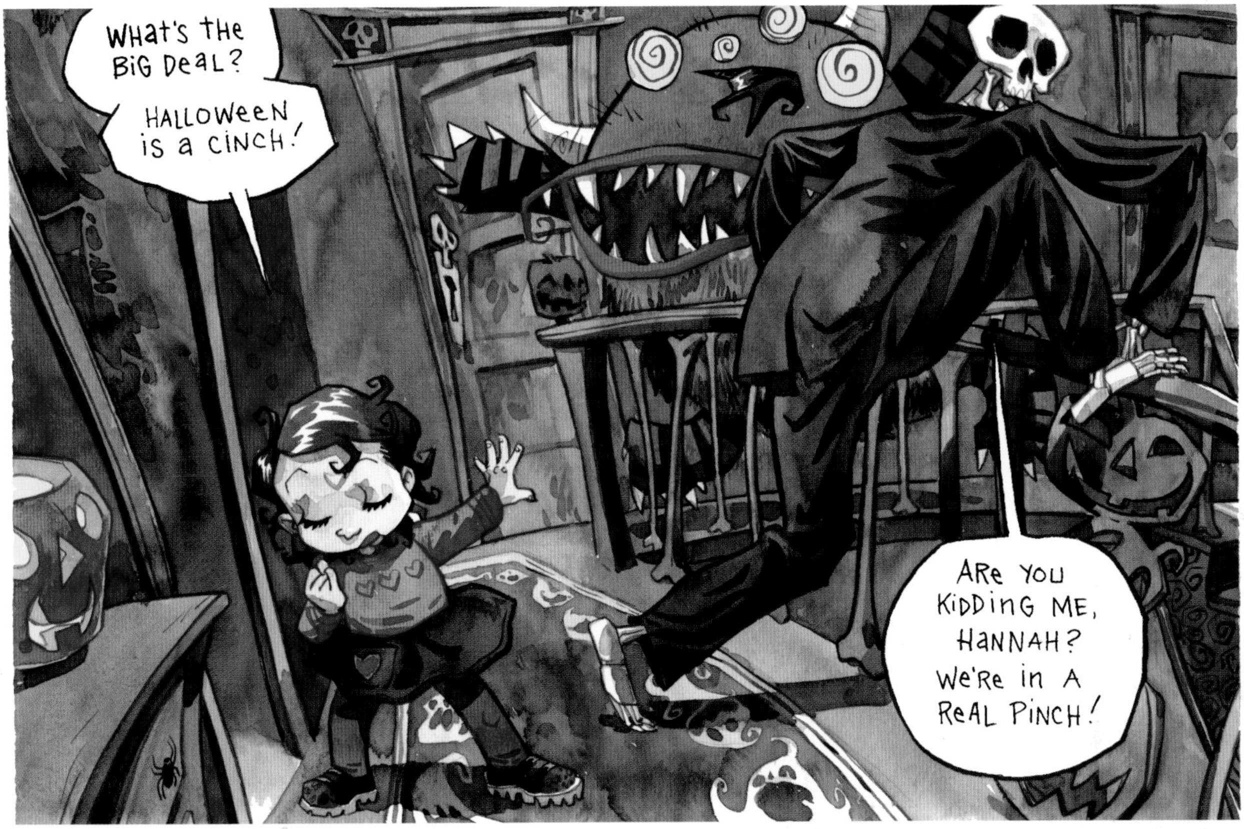
What's the Big Deal?
HALLOWEEN is a CINCH!
ARe YOU KIDDING ME, HANNAH? We'Re in A ReAL PINCH!

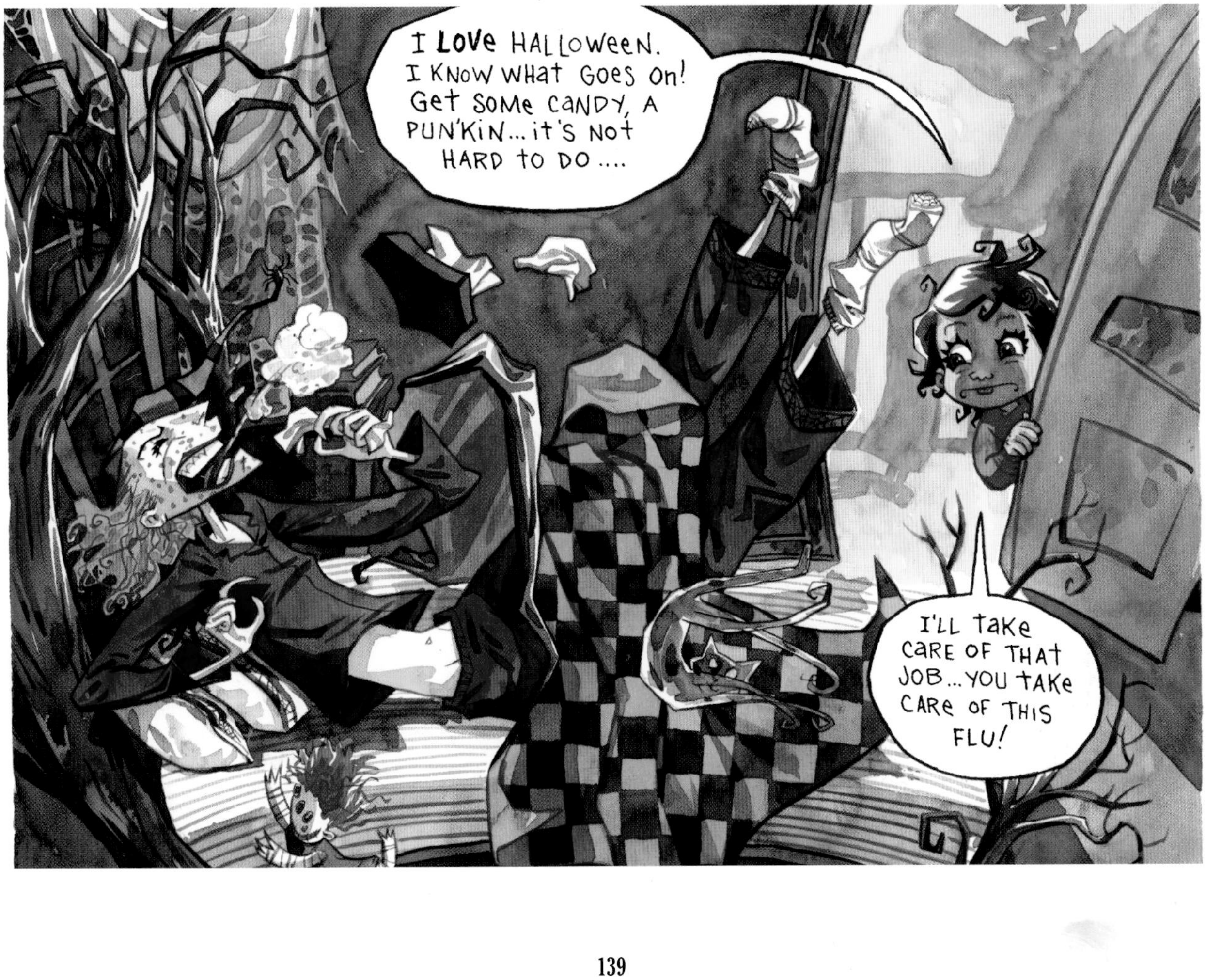
I LOVE HALLOWEEN. I KNOW WHAT GOES On! Get SOMe CANDY, A PUN'KIN... it's NOT HARD TO DO....
I'LL TAKE CARE OF THAT JOB...YOU TAKE CARE OF THIS FLU!

So her pals dressed her up in a tutu and hat. She was handed a list and a broom and a cat . . .
a thermos and lunch, a bag of supplies, and then Hannah Marie took off to the night skies!

As she zoomed up into the indigo blue, she heard Mr. Pettibone (and Bug-A-Boo, too . . .)

When Hannah checked out her list, she was shocked and surprised . . .
at the number of tasks and the paper's long size.

She started her work snagging ghosts, shrieks, and moans.

She constructed a Scarecrow using sticks as the bones.

She assigned all the phantoms to their Haunted House spaces . . .

. . . and she scattered dry leaves to the tree-deprived places!

She crocheted fresh cobwebs . . .

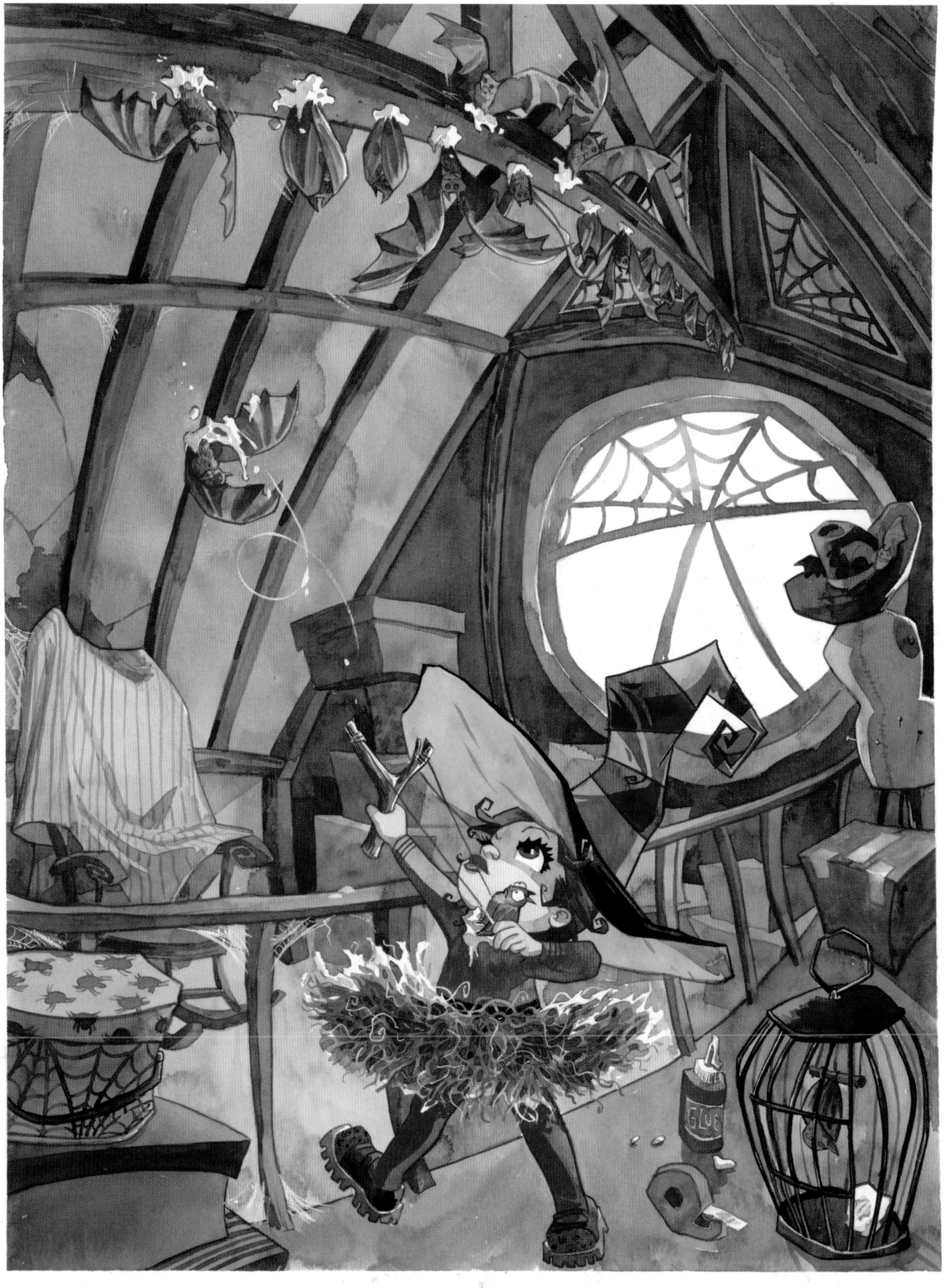
GLUE

She belfreyed the bats . . .

She vacuumed the arches in Halloween cats.

She coaxed the storm clouds out of warm autumn breezes . . .

. . . while Pettibone treated Scary's horrible sneezes!

She conducted a chorus of full moon wolf howls.

She set monster jaws into fierce, toothy scowls.

She poked her poor thumb sewing on monster parts.

And one needs to take care during the electric kick start!

153

With time running out, and so much at stake, she didn't have time for her unionized breaks!

It's hard to eat sandwiches by the light of the moon . . .
or sip slurps of soup while you're riding a broom!

She wised up the owls . . .

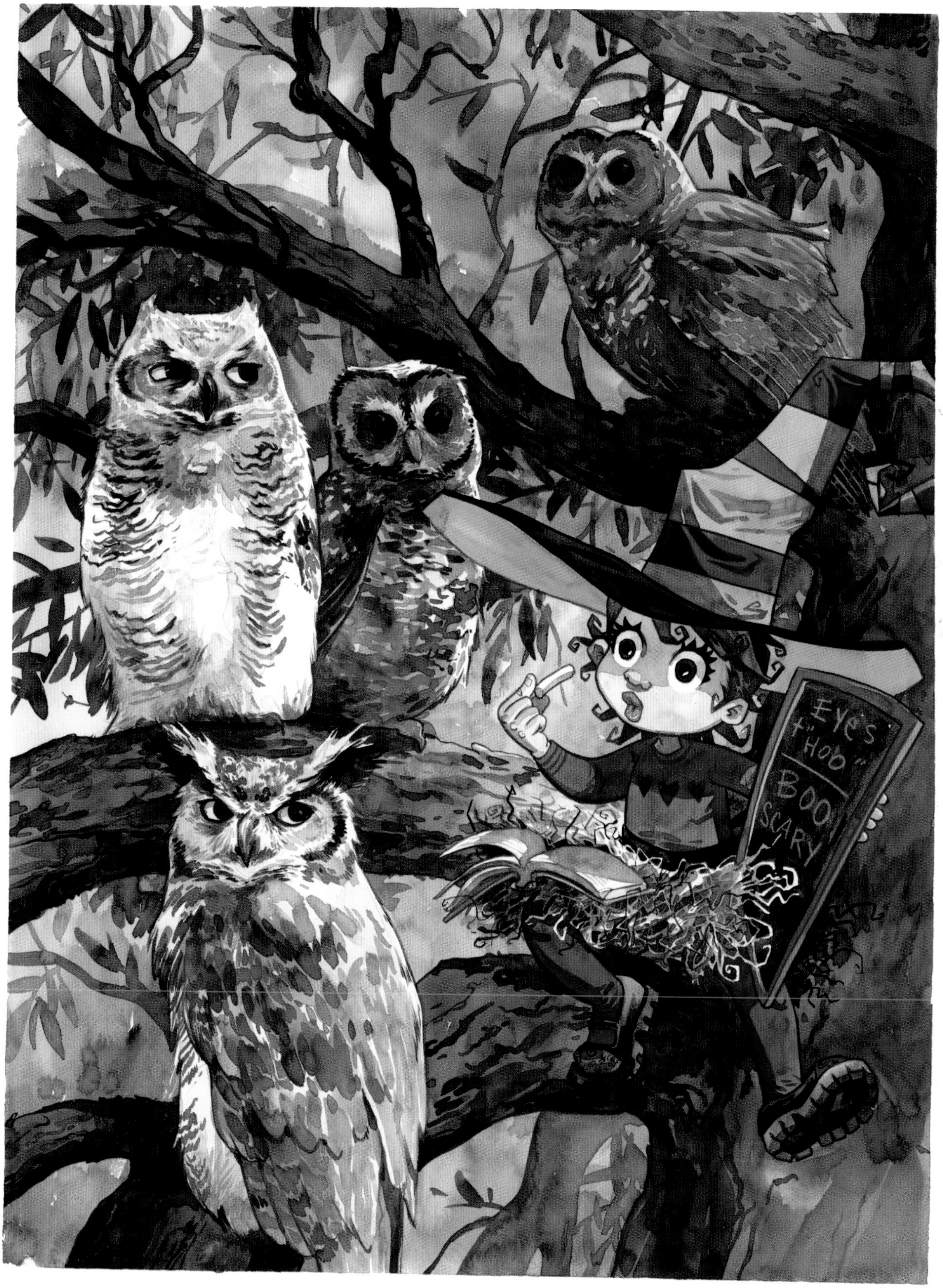
Eye's
+ "Hoo"
BOO
SCARY

She wrapped up a mummy . . .

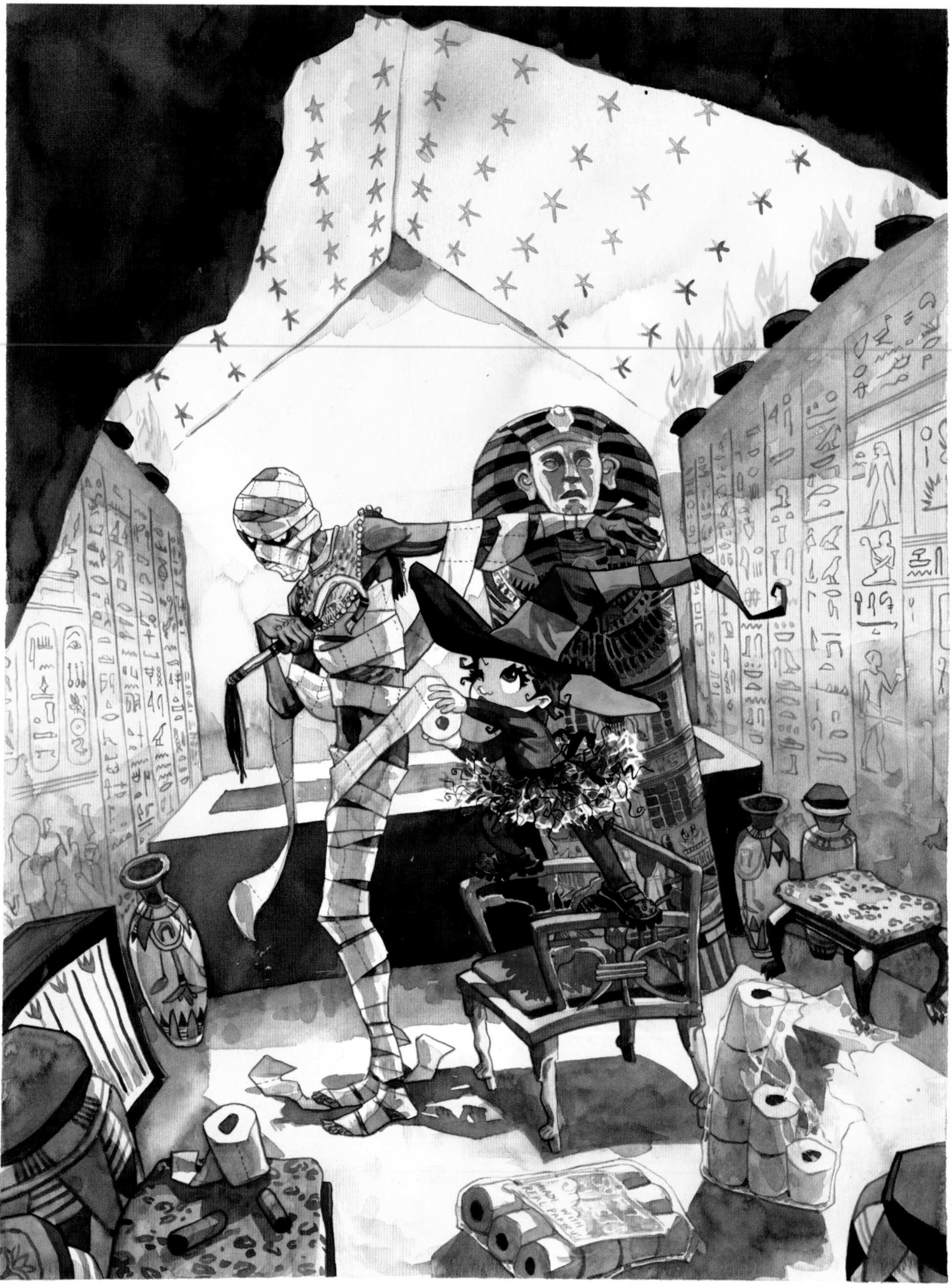

She delivered some takeout for sea monsters' tummies.

But when she arrived at the old pumpkin patch . . .

. . . the substitute godmother had met her match!

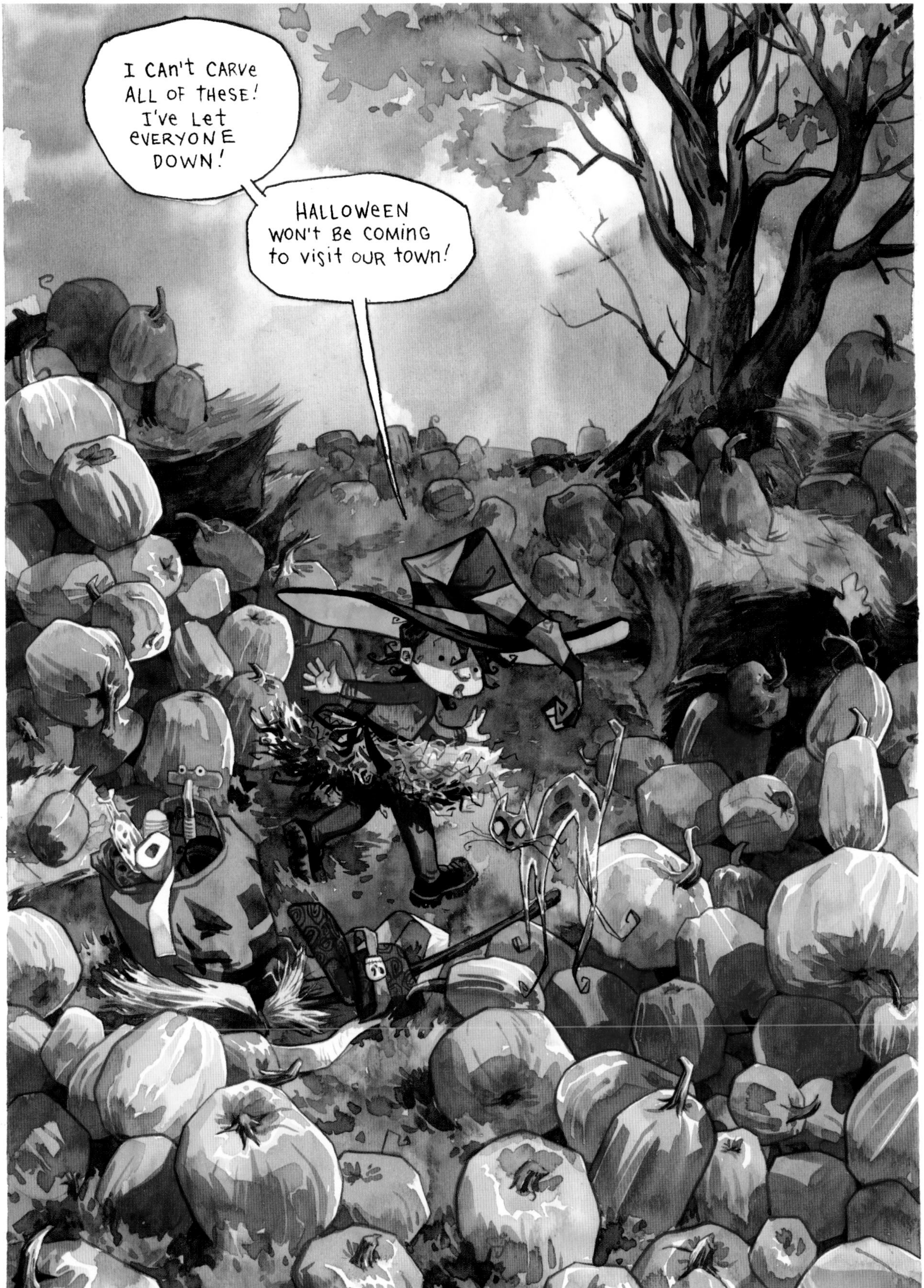
I CAN'T CARVE ALL OF THESE! I'VE LET EVERYONE DOWN!
HALLOWEEN WON'T BE COMING TO VISIT OUR TOWN!

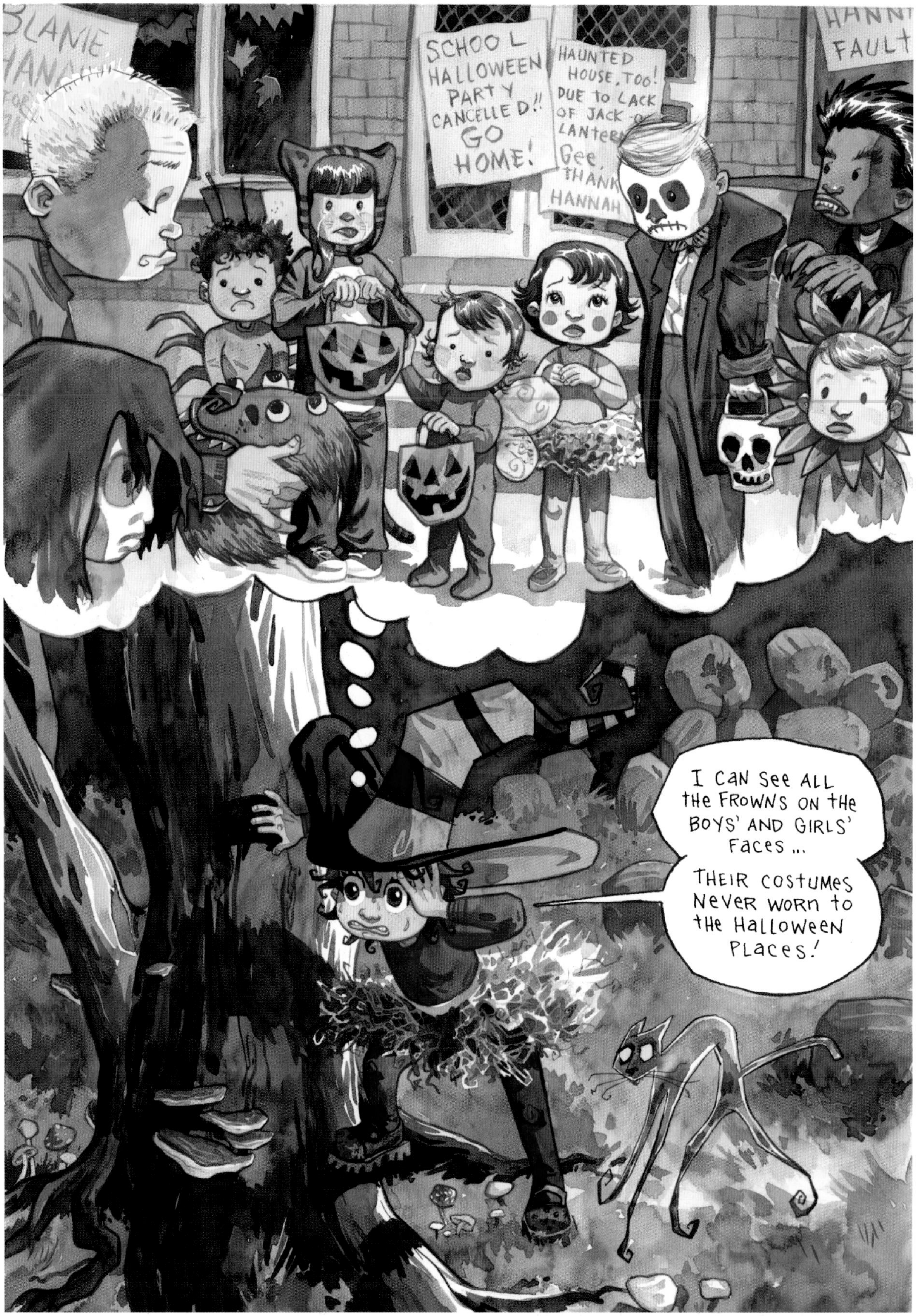
BLAME HANNA
SCHOOL HALLOWEEN PARTY CANCELLED!! GO HOME!
HAUNTED HOUSE, TOO! DUE TO LACK OF JACK-O LANTERN
Gee, THANKS HANNAH
FAULT
I CAN SEE ALL THE FROWNS ON THE BOYS' AND GIRLS' FACES...
THEIR COSTUMES NEVER WORN TO THE HALLOWEEN PLACES!

Hannah's eyes began leaking. She made loud sobbing sounds.
She caused Orson the vampire to wake in the ground!

The Vampire family caused much dirt to scatter as they decoffined themselves to see
what was the matter (to see Hannah's tears would cause most hearts to shatter!).

But these are the vampires, used to sounds of sad weeping.
Their concern extends to the quality of their sleeping!

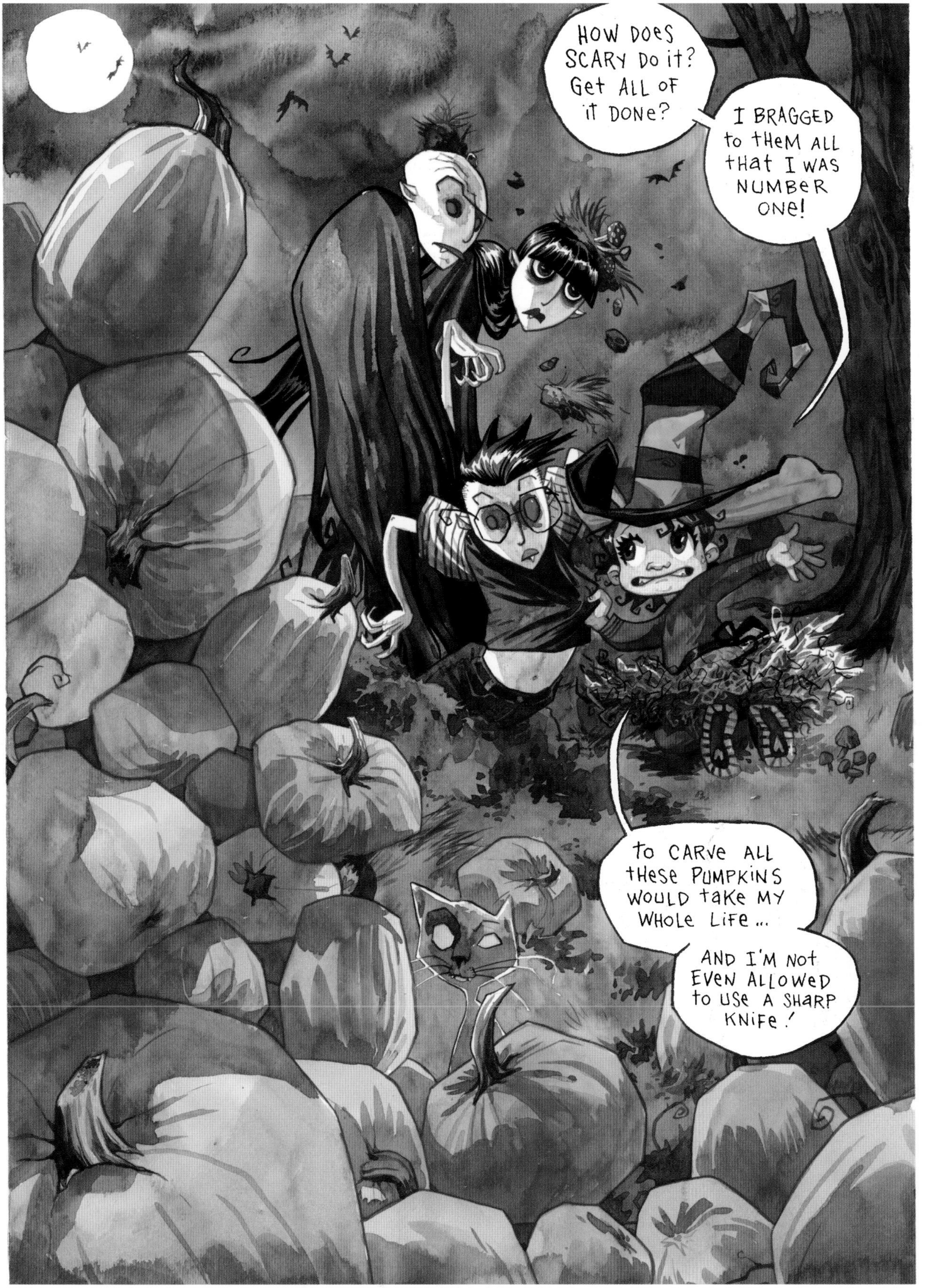
HOW DOES SCARY DO it? Get ALL OF it DONE?
I BRAGGED to tHeM ALL that I WAS NUMBER ONE!
to CARVE ALL tHese PUMPKINS WOULD take MY WHOLe LIFe...
AND I'M Not EVEN ALLOWED to USe A SHARP KNIFe!

The Vampires laughed with sharp, pointy grins.

And that's just what they did, all through the night.
They chewed jack-o'-lanterns with monstrous delight!

Back at Scary's bedside, progress was made. Professor Toad
was called to administer an olde-tyme healing aid!

Soon the Boo Flu was vanquished, all pox, shakes, and sneezes!
No longer did her lungs make rattling wheezes!

With all sickness banished from her haunted hair . . . Scary Godmother quickly took to the air!

With three pumpkins remaining, the vamps widened their eyes.

They scrambled back into their earth-covered beds,
as Halloween sun kissed our girl's weary head.

A sleep-deprived Hannah cast her eyes to the street.
She twiddled her fingers and shuffled her feet.

Scary Godmother just laughed—a magical sound!

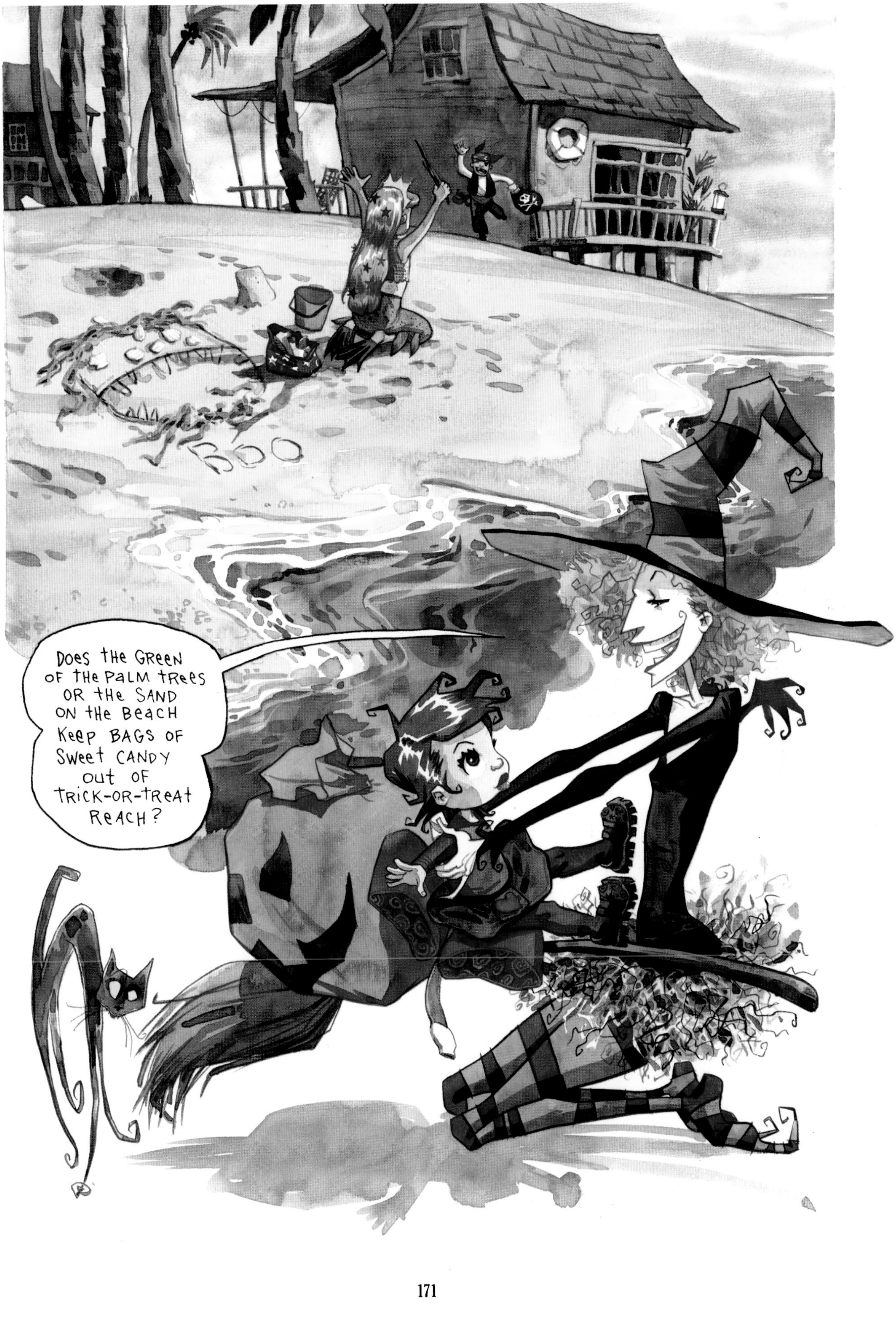
BOO
DOES THE GREEN OF THE PALM TREES OR THE SAND ON THE BEACH KEEP BAGS OF SWEET CANDY OUT OF TRICK-OR-TREAT REACH?

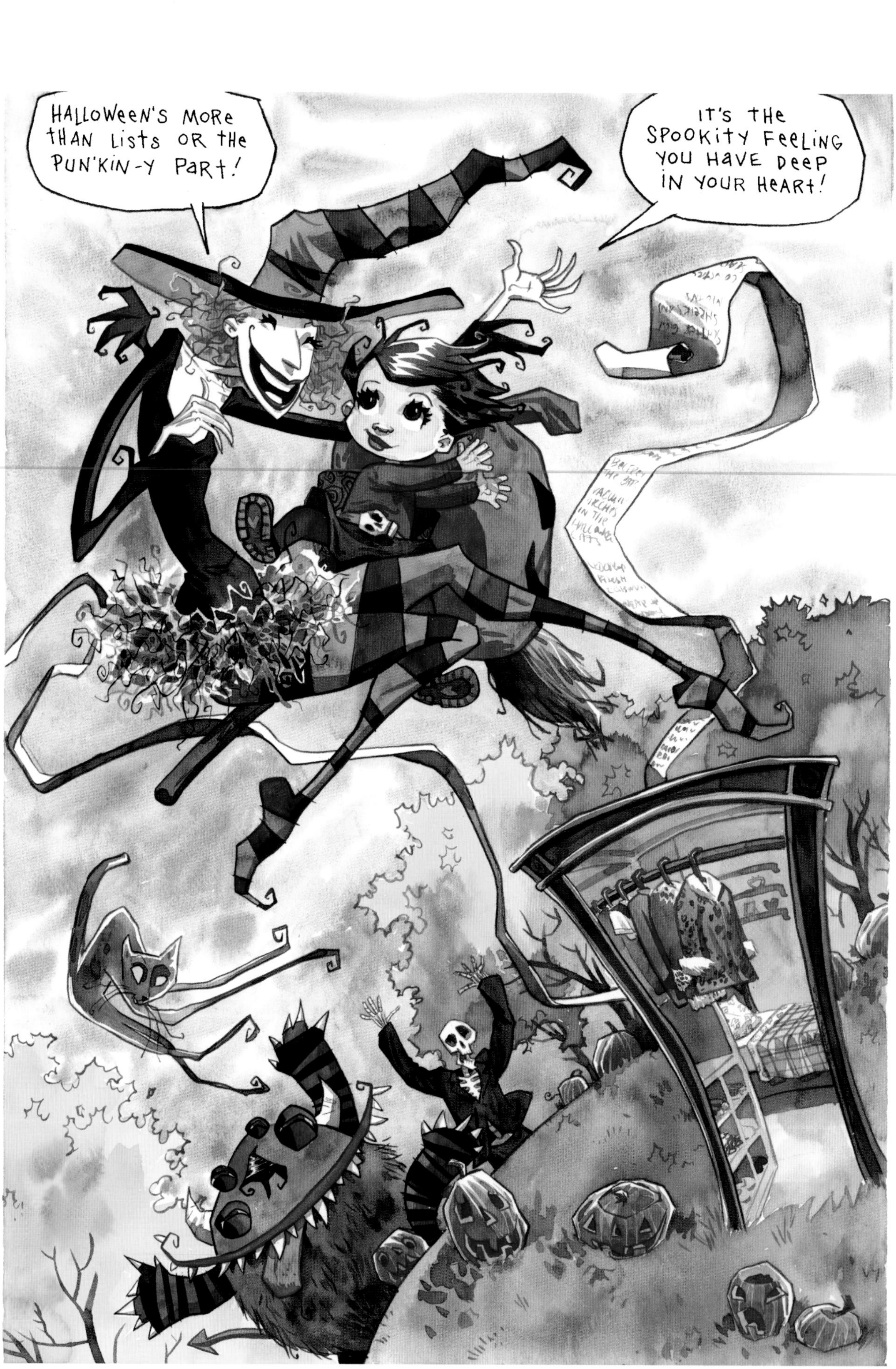
HALLOWEEN'S MORE THAN LISTS OR THE PUN'KIN-Y PART!
IT'S THE SPOOKITY FEELING YOU HAVE DEEP IN YOUR HEART!

"With long, purple shadows, a good chill up your spine;
that heart-racing feeling comes from me here and mine!"

"Halloween comes to you on Monster feet—creeping!"

And how did Hannah celebrate her Halloween?

By sleeping!

THE END

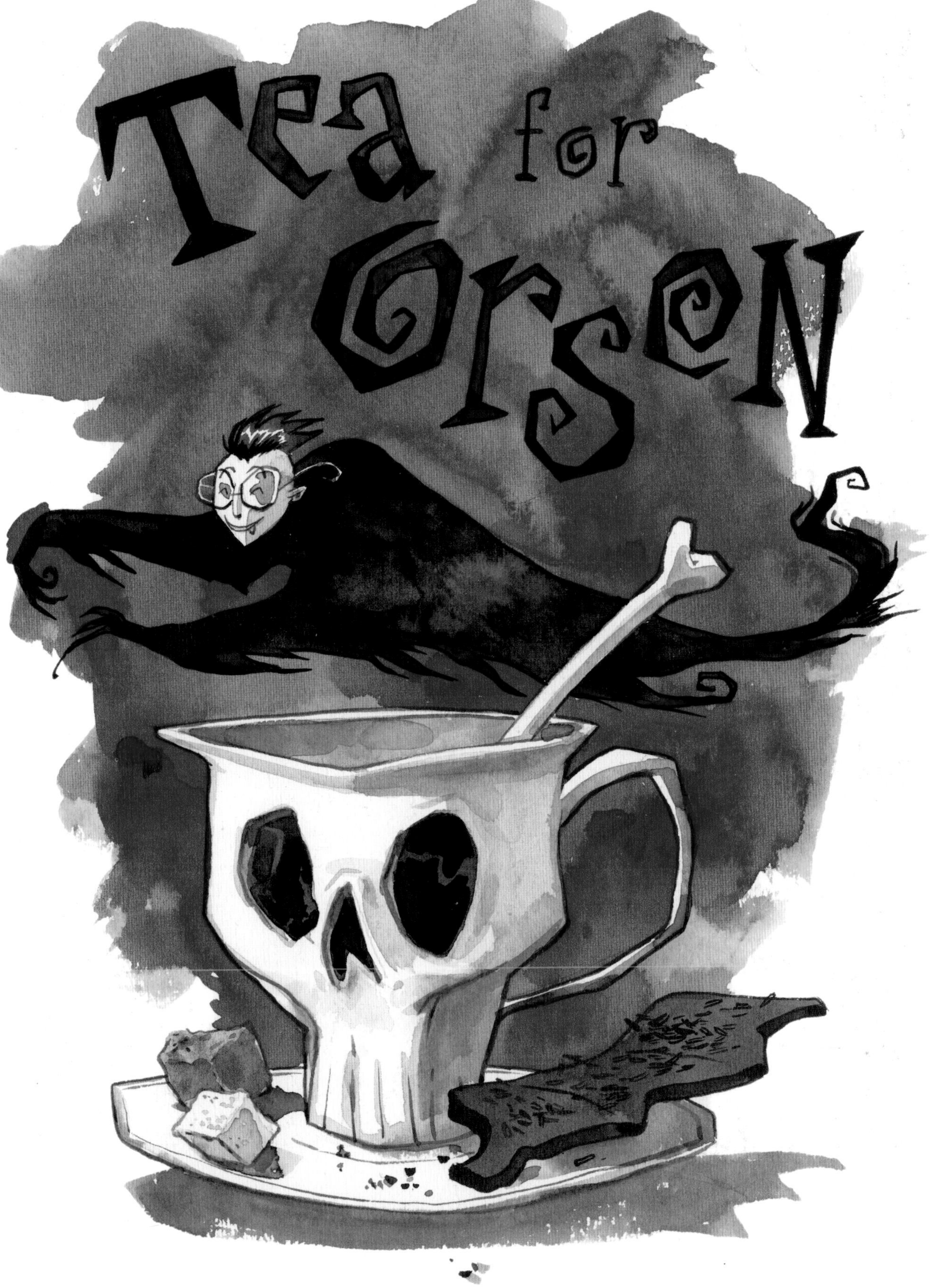
Tea for Orson

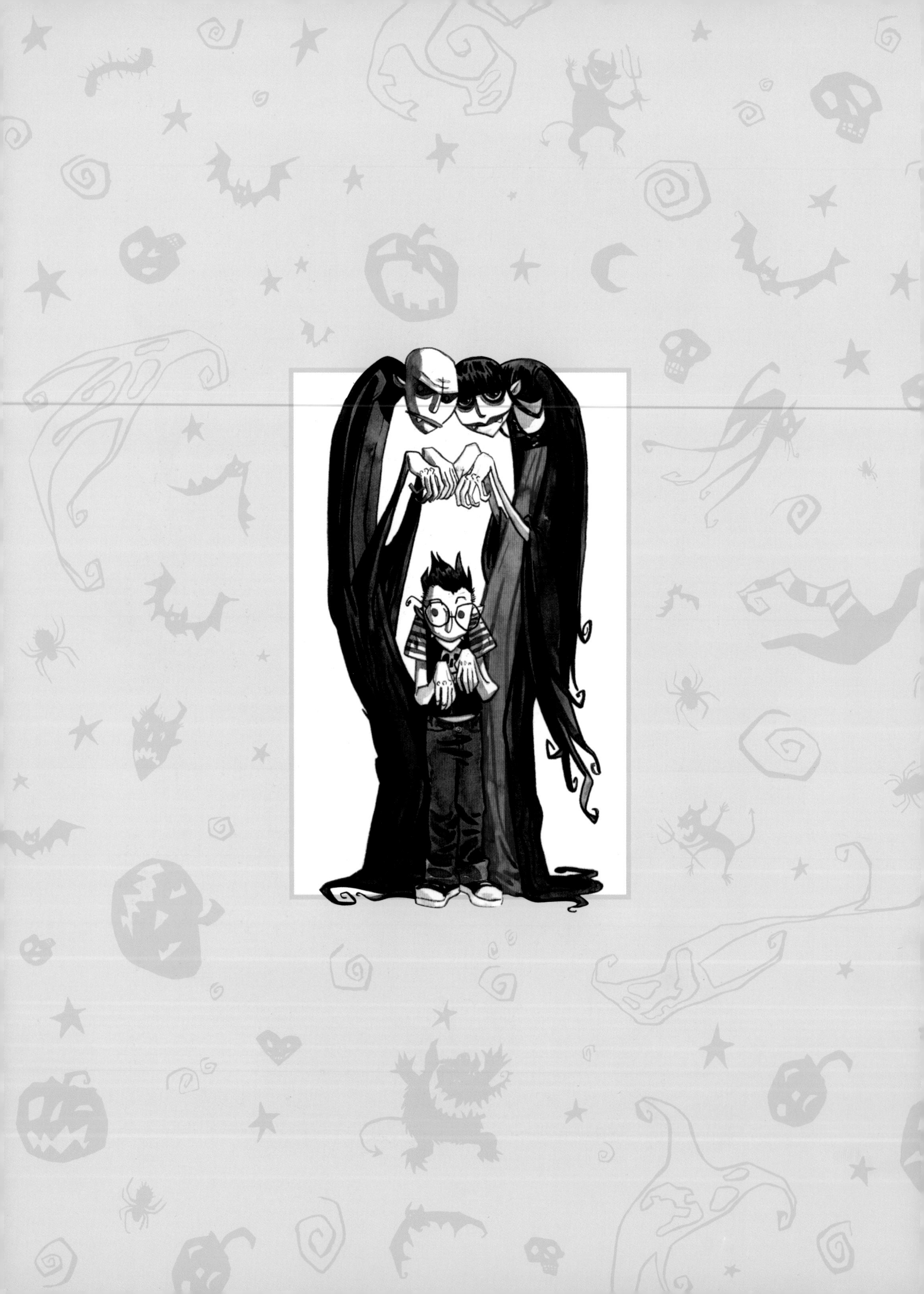

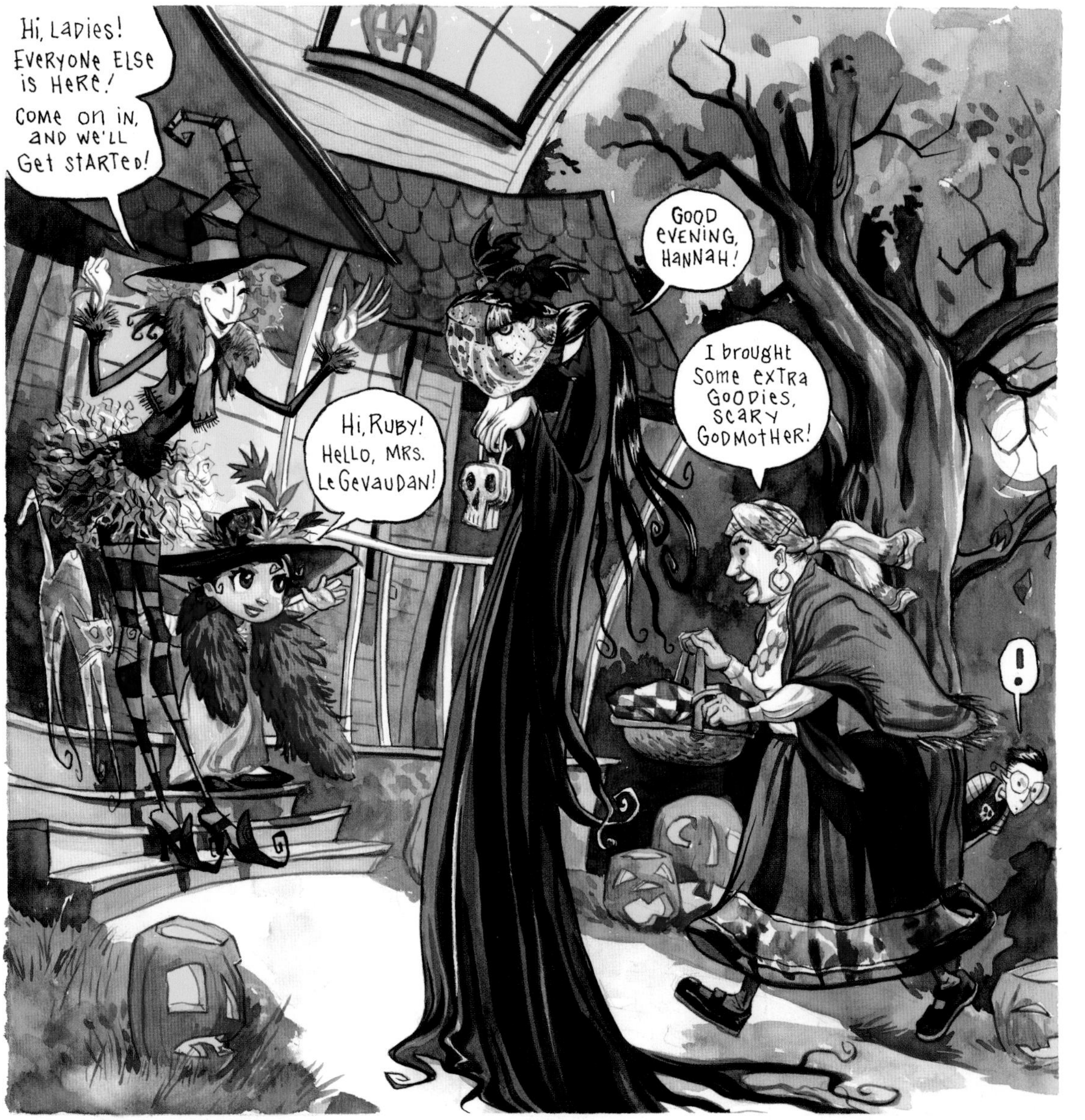
Hi, Ladies! Everyone Else is Here! Come on in, and we'll Get started!
Good evening, Hannah!
I brought some extra Goodies, scary Godmother!
Hi, Ruby! Hello, Mrs. LeGevaudan!
!

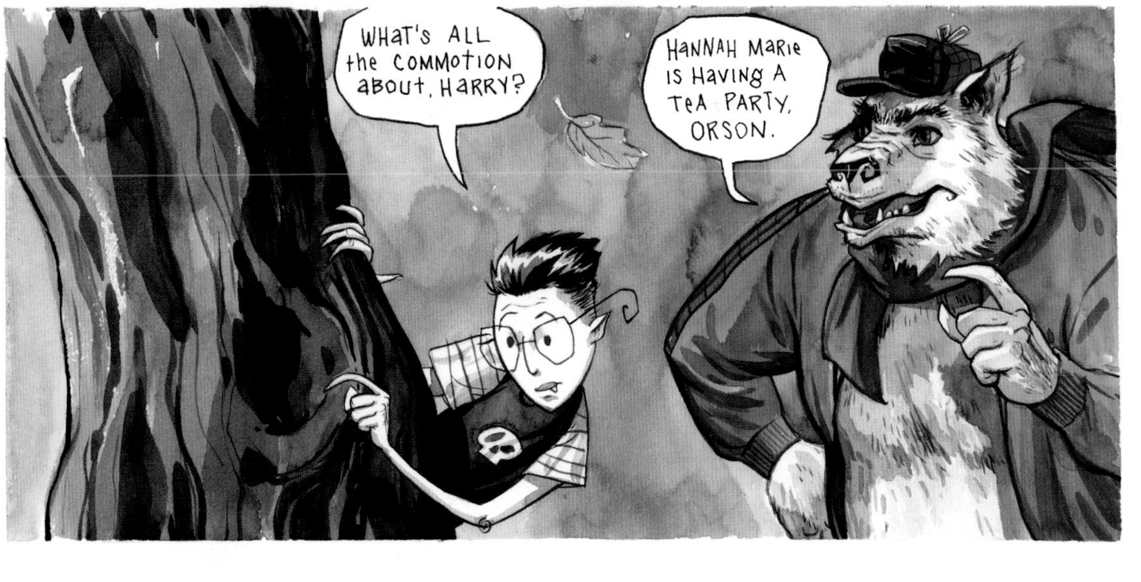
What's all the commotion about, Harry?
Hannah Marie is Having a Tea Party, Orson.

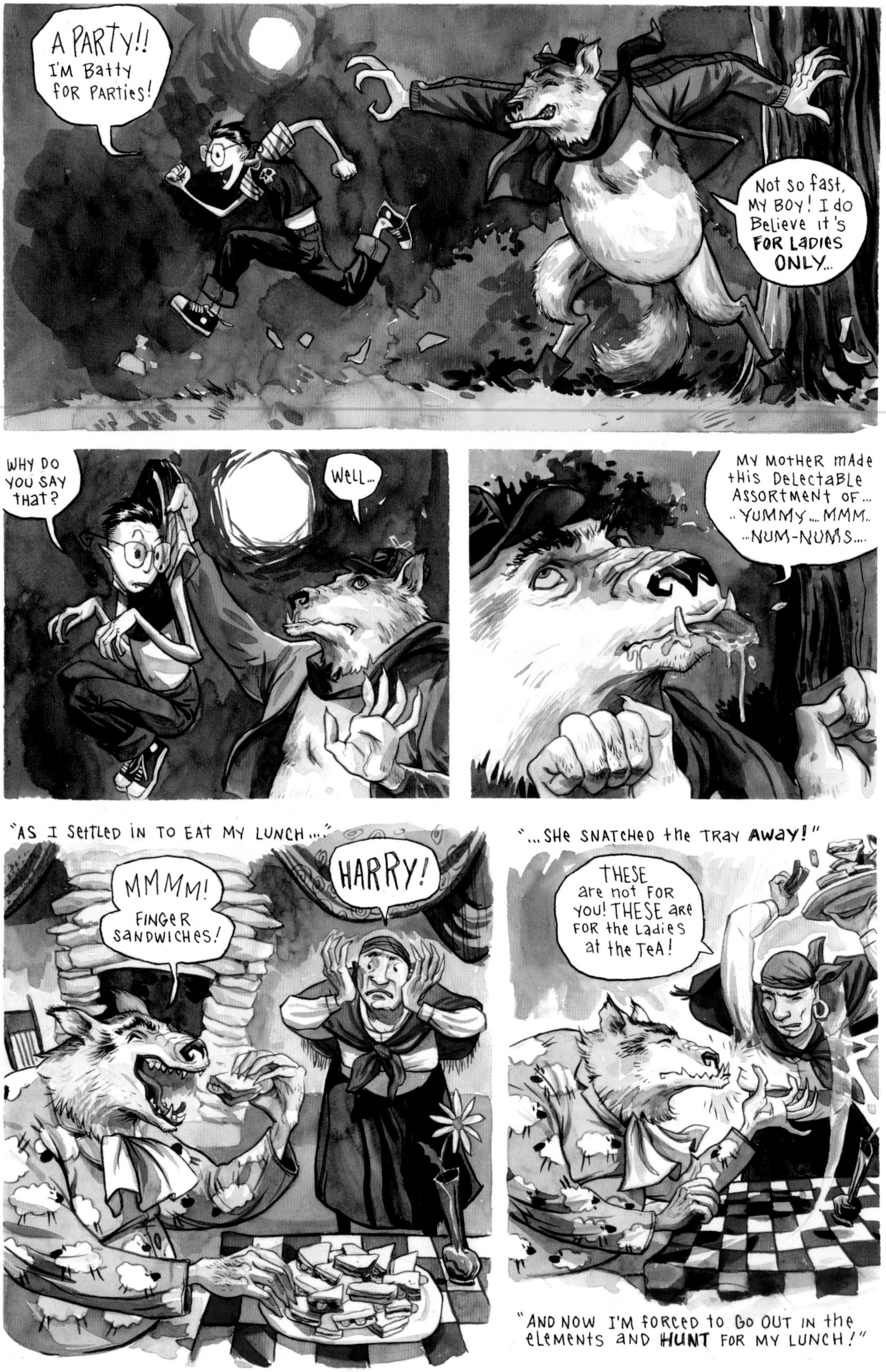
A PARTY!! I'M Batty FOR PARTIES!
Not so fast, MY BOY! I do Believe it's FOR LADIES ONLY...
WHY DO YOU SAY THAT?
WELL...
MY MOTHER MADE THIS DELECTABLE ASSORTMENT OF... ..YUMMY.... MMM.. ..NUM-NUMS....
"AS I SETTLED IN TO EAT MY LUNCH..."
MMMM! FINGER SANDWICHES!
HARRY!
"...SHE SNATCHED THE TRAY AWAY!"
THESE are not FOR you! THESE are FOR the Ladies at the TEA!
"AND NOW I'M FORCED TO GO OUT IN THE ELEMENTS AND HUNT FOR MY LUNCH!"

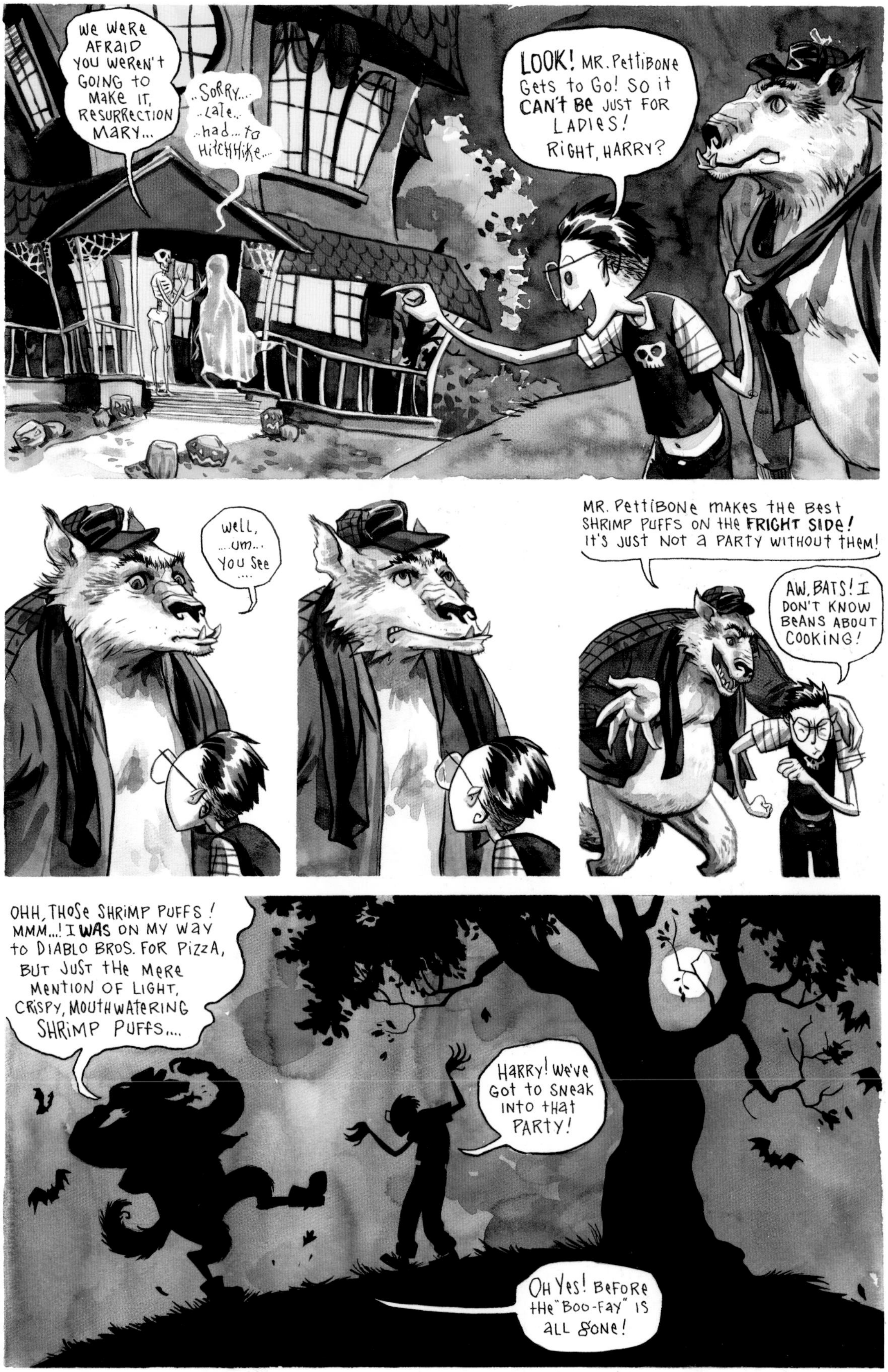
We were afraid you weren't going to make it, Resurrection Mary...
..Sorry... ..late.. ..had... to hitchhike.....
LOOK! Mr. Pettibone gets to go! So it CAN'T BE just for ladies! Right, Harry?
Well, ...um... you see ....
Mr. Pettibone makes the best shrimp puffs on the FRIGHT SIDE! It's just not a party without them!
Aw, bats! I don't know beans about cooking!
Ohh, those shrimp puffs! Mmm...! I WAS on my way to Diablo Bros. for pizza, but just the mere mention of light, crispy, mouthwatering shrimp puffs....
Harry! We've got to sneak into that party!
Oh yes! Before the "Boo-Fay" is all gone!

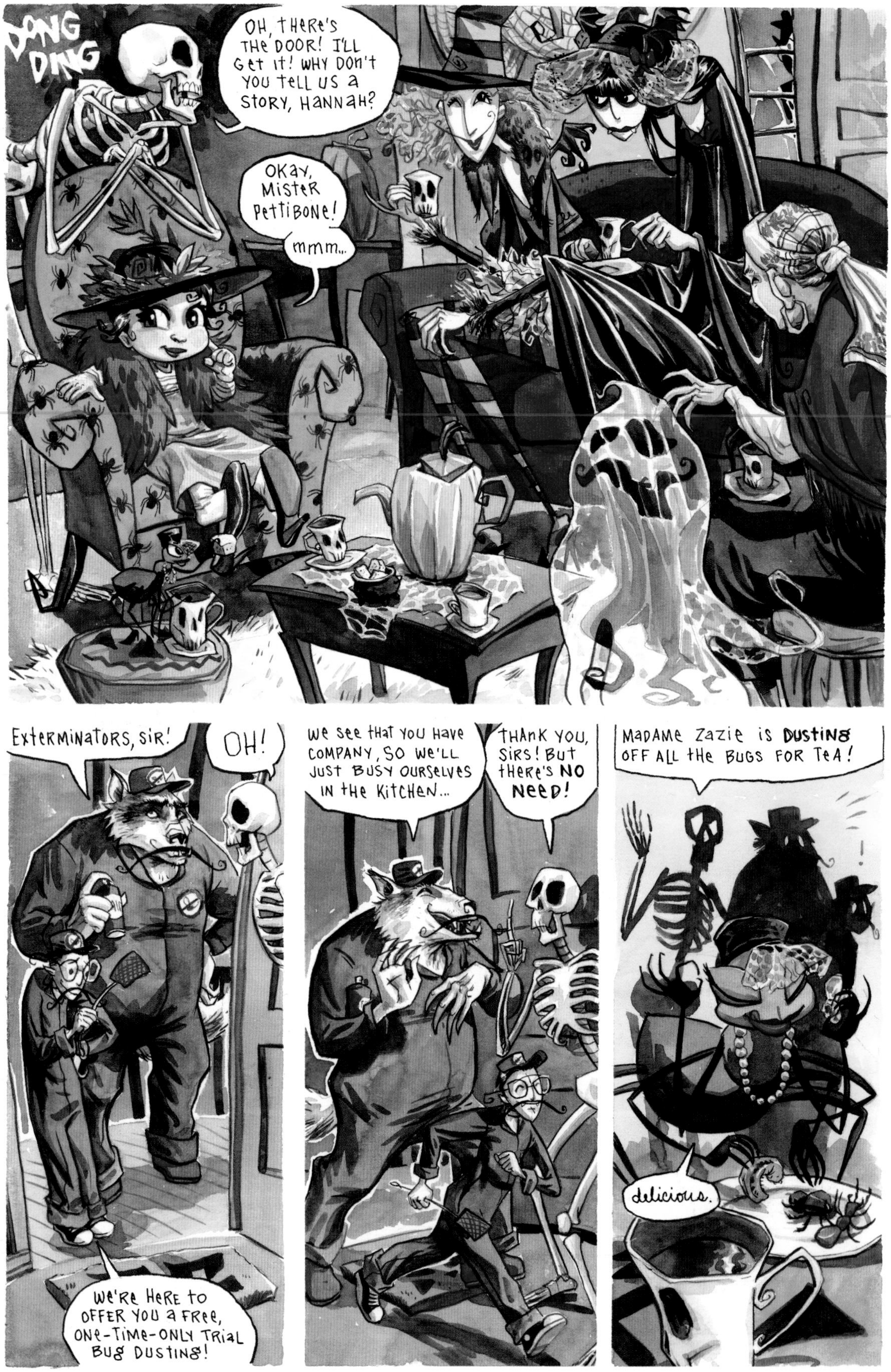
DONG DING
OH, THERE'S THE DOOR! I'LL GET IT! WHY DON'T YOU TELL US A STORY, HANNAH?
OKAY, MISTER PETTIBONE!
mmm...
EXTERMINATORS, SIR!
OH!
WE'RE HERE TO OFFER YOU A FREE, ONE-TIME-ONLY TRIAL BUG DUSTING!
WE SEE THAT YOU HAVE COMPANY, SO WE'LL JUST BUSY OURSELVES IN THE KITCHEN...
THANK YOU, SIRS! BUT THERE'S NO NEED!
MADAME ZAZIE IS DUSTING OFF ALL THE BUGS FOR TEA!
delicious.

AND SO~

OOF!

ALL THAT **HORRIBLE** CLIMBING!! I'M NOT ONE FOR SPORT, YOU KNOW..

AND **THIS** IS WHAT COMES OF IT?

~YEESH~ STOP WHINING AND **HELP** ME!

PUSH!

SO, HANNAH SAID HE **ZIPS** DOWN AND UP **EVERYONE'S** CHIMNEY IN ONE NIGHT? HA!

AAARR!!

C'MON, HARRY! WIGGLE YOUR LEGS!

WELL, HE **CERTAINLY** MUST BE A **SVELTE** FELLOW!

SLENDER! PETITE, EVEN...

AND THEN~

?

JUMP A LITTLE!

I AM!

FLAP YOUR WINGS, BOY! PUT A LITTLE **EFFORT** INTO IT!

!

YOU'RE **TOO** HEAVY! IT'S NO USE!

WE'RE **ALMOST** THERE! THAT OPEN WINDOW IS **NEARLY** IN MY REACH.

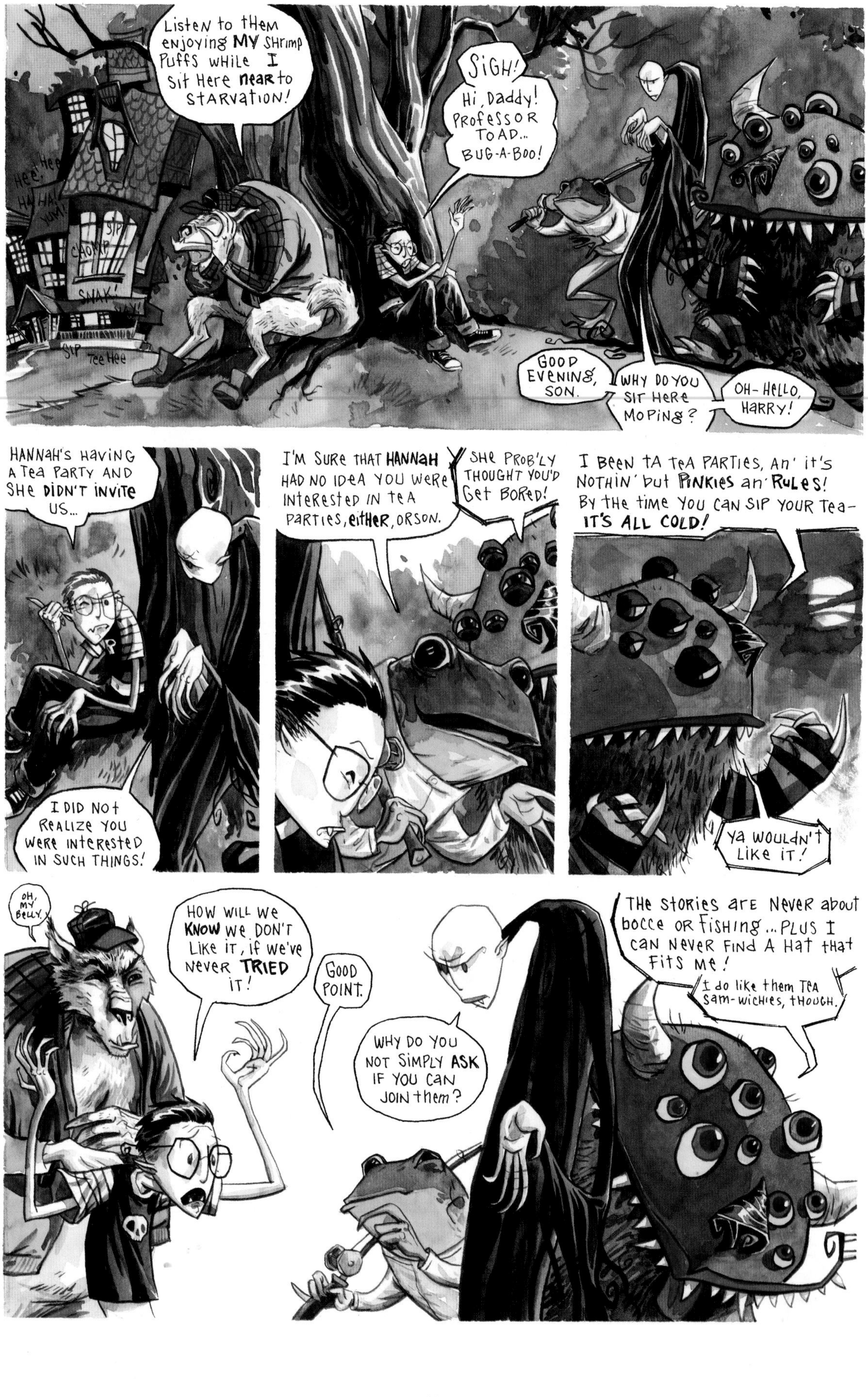

Listen to tHem enjoying MY SHrimp Puffs wHile I sit Here near to starvation!
SIGH!
Hi, Daddy! Professor Toad... Bug-a-Boo!
SNAK!
Tee Hee
Good evening, son.
Why do you sit here moping?
Oh- Hello, Harry!
Hannah's having a tea party and she didn't invite us...
I did not realize you were interested in such things!
I'm sure that Hannah had no idea you were interested in tea parties, either, Orson.
She prob'ly thought you'd get bored!
I been ta tea parties, an' it's nothin' but pinkies an' rules! By the time you can sip your tea- it's all cold!
Ya wouldn't like it!
Oh, my belly.
How will we know we don't like it, if we've never tried it!
Good point.
Why do you not simply ask if you can join them?
The stories are never about bocce or fishing... plus I can never find a hat that fits me!
I do like them tea sam-wichies, though.

WELL, HERE GOES NOTHIN'!

DONG DING

POK!

CREAK!

ASK POLITELY!

OKAY.

ORSON! HARRY!

HOY, HOY, FELLOWS! WHAT CAN I DO FOR YOU?

HI, MR. PETTIBONE... UM... ME AND HARRY... CAN... WE ...PLEASE COME TO YOUR PARTY?

FIRST OF ALL, YOU NEED SOME APPROPRIATE TEA CLOTHES! THEN, WE'LL BONE UP ON ETIQUETTE!

LADIES! WE HAVE SOME LATE ARRIVALS!

GET YOURSELVES SOME CAKES AND SAVORIES AND I'LL FETCH YOU SOME TEA!

LOOK AT THAT GASTRONOMICAL BOUNTY, BOY!

FOOD, SHMOOD! I'M READY TO PLAY SOME GAMES!

AND SO the SMALL PIG RAN AWAY AND HE
INTO HIS NOSE AND A FROG IS ON his H
TAIL! AND then A SNAKE SAYS THIS IS O
TO A JUNKYARD AND HE THINK
AND EMPTY CANS BUT NO M
AND HE'S SCARED OF
AND HE SEES SOME
MUD AND
VACUUM C
THINKS it's
stare
WHAT A PIP THAT PIG IS... HA!
I WONDER IF there are any bacon sandwiches, Orson..
there must be, 'cause this story is like chewin' on gristle! It goes on and on ....
RUNS
CITY
MUD...
AND ON...
AND WHEN HE OPENED UP HIS MOUTH....
HE DIDN'T HAVE A FACE!
BIG DEAL! I KNOW LOTS OF GUYS WHO DON'T HAVE a FACE!
And ON...
MARY, YOU'RE POSITIVELY TRANSLUCENT tonight!
YOU MUST BE IN LOVE!
OH YES...!
involved ... in new... Love.... Affair.... tell you.... ALL ABOUT ...HIM... He's....recently deceased....
AND ON AND ON AND ON....!
ZE LOCUSTS ARE IMPORTED.
STUFFED WITH A MIX OF...
MUST GET YOUR RECIPE!
TWO OUNDS OF EBALLS!
MY COMPLIMENTS ON THE BOO-FAY! NARF! CHOMP!

MANY MANY STORIES LATER

tick

I CAN'T BELIEVE I WANTED TO COME TO THIS STUPID PARTY....

NOT YOUR "CUP OF TEA," EH, ORSON?

SCARY GODMOTHER! SORRY!

I DIDN'T... I MEAN... IT'S NOT... I... UM... TEA...

ACTUALLY, I DON'T THINK I COULD HANDLE **another** CUP OF TEA, EITHER!

WOULD **YOU** LIKE TO TELL US THE **NEXT** STORY?

OKAY!

HOW HUMOROUS!! THAT **REMINDS** ME...

UMF... OF THE ORIGIN EPISODE OF "CRYPTO" THE DEVIL DOG ON "THE SPECTRAL SIX"...

Chomp!

OH NO.

WHAT'S "THE SPECTRAL SIX"?

SMEK! OH MY! YOU'VE **NEVER** SEEN "THE SPECTRAL SIX"?

LUCKY FOR YOU... I HAVE COMMITTED THEM **ALL** TO MEMORY!

ALLOW ME TO BRING YOU UP TO SPEED! EPISODE #1- INTRODUCED US TO OUR FAIR HEROINE, MISS CRYSTAL

... HER EYES ROLL UP AND BACK INTO HER HEAD! UNBEKNOWNST TO HER CAPTORS, MISS CRYSTAL WAS POSSESSED BY THE ECTOPLASM TWINS! THEY BELIEVED SHE HAD FAINTED AND LAUGHED AT HER PERCEIVED FRAILTY!
.... COVER OF THE MOONLESS SKY, THE TWINS LEVITATED HER OUT OF THE HORRIBLE PIT!
.... WHEN THE VILLAINS ENTERED THE PIT THE NEXT MORNING, THEY WERE GREETED BY THE FEARSOME FORM OF THE CIVIL WARRIOR
WITH THE HELP OF MUERTO RICO, HE HAD TUNNELED... A... WAY...
Zz
ZAWK
CLATTER
ASLEEP! WITH BELLIES FULL, NO DOUBT! THE "BOO-FAY" IS GONE AND THE DINNER HOUR IS NEAR! HOW ILL PLANNED THIS PARTY IS! I MUST PROVIDE FOR MYSELF! PERHAPS SCARY GODMOTHER HAS AN ACCOUNT AT DIABLO BROS. PIZZA?
Z.
Z
ZAZZ
SOME WEEKS LATER...
$!
SKULLY, DO YOU REMEMBER ORDERING THE DANTE'S INFERNO SPECIAL FROM DIABLO BROTHERS?
BILL
EEE! THAT'S A TOPPING FROM EVERY CIRCLE OF HELL! I DON'T HAVE THE STOMACH FOR IT!
END.

SCARY GODMOTHER
SketchBook

Hi, everybody! Welcome to the sketchbook.
I'm Jill, and I'll be your guide today!

Here in the cleverly named 'Scary Godmother Sketchbook,'
you'll see as much art as we could pack in here from the
first printings of the collectible, rare, and wonderful Sirius
Entertainment editions of the Scary Godmother books!

Above our talky-talking we have art from the credits page
of *The Mystery Date*! Below is art I made up to plug
my signings and appearances at conventions!

ON THE ROAD

Well, let's go clockwise, shall we? And look! It's the first, black-and-white drawing I made of Scary Godmother and the Boozle from just a marker skritch-scratch on Bristol board.

Next we have the second, full-color illustration I did of Scary Godmother, Hannah, and Bug-A-Boo (who thankfully did not stay in that chicken/goblin incarnation). And that bat with the glasses? He soon became Orson, Prince of the Night, and Hannah's vampire pal!

Rounding the page out is an illustration from the stationery set Sirius made! I still have one—*how 'bout you?*

— SCARY GODMOTHER
and BOOZLE the ghost —

Above you will see the first drawing of Hannah! Yes, the first—for true! Moving over a little, we have an older version of Hannah, requested by the folks at Mainframe Entertainment, who made the animated *Scary Godmother* specials.

Above, you'll see an ad piece for *Scary Godmother* that I did for Sirius to promote our first book! Bug-A-Boo was shaping up, but Orson was still a bat! I believe I called him "Blind as a Bat."

Above are expression sheets of Hannah and Scary Godmother that I did for the animators at Mainframe Entertainment. Above and to the right is one of the original illustrations I did when I was pitching *Scary Godmother* to all the book and comics publishers.

Jimmy   Katy

Here we have our misguided villain, Jimmy. He's not a bad kid, just a bit self-involved. But he makes a good heel, doesn't he? Why? Because he believes that he is right! He's based on many of the traits of my older cousin Jimmy, who used to scare the bejeezus out of us younger kids, just cuz he could. There's a bit of the Grinch in Jimmy, too, cuz I loves the Grinch!

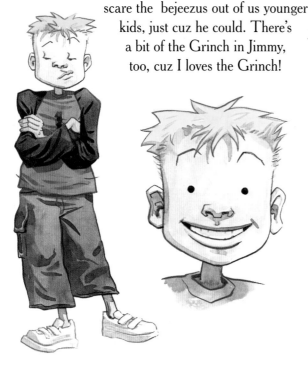

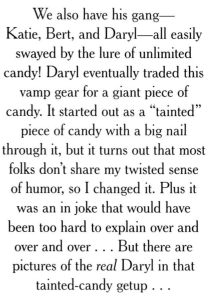

Bert   Daryl

We also have his gang— Katie, Bert, and Daryl—all easily swayed by the lure of unlimited candy! Daryl eventually traded this vamp gear for a giant piece of candy. It started out as a "tainted" piece of candy with a big nail through it, but it turns out that most folks don't share my twisted sense of humor, so I changed it. Plus it was an in joke that would have been too hard to explain over and over and over . . . But there are pictures of the *real* Daryl in that tainted-candy getup . . .

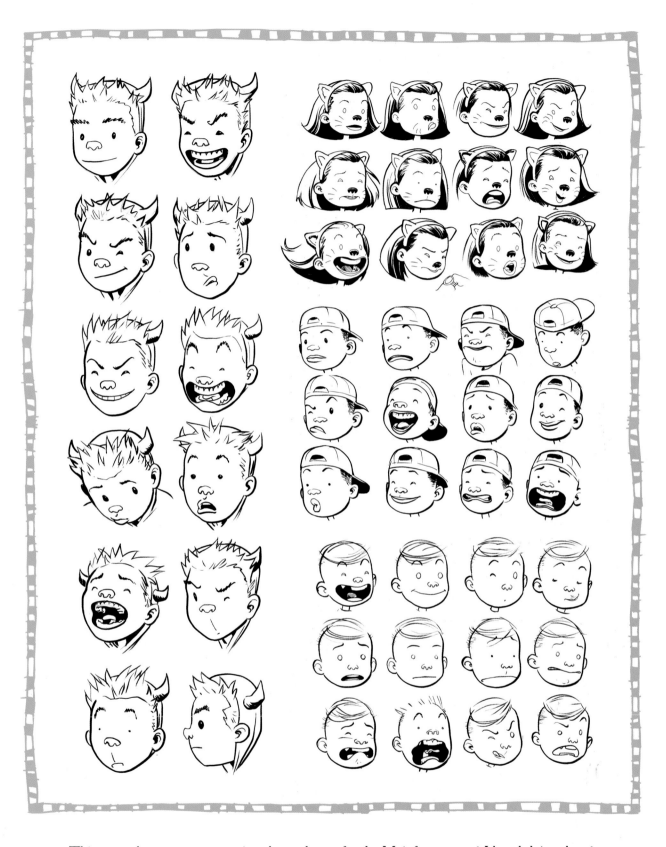

This page shows more expression sheets drawn for the Mainframe gang! I loved doing these!
It was great working with director Ezekiel Norton and the wonderful animators! The following
pages feature the wraparound cover for the original *Scary Godmother* book.

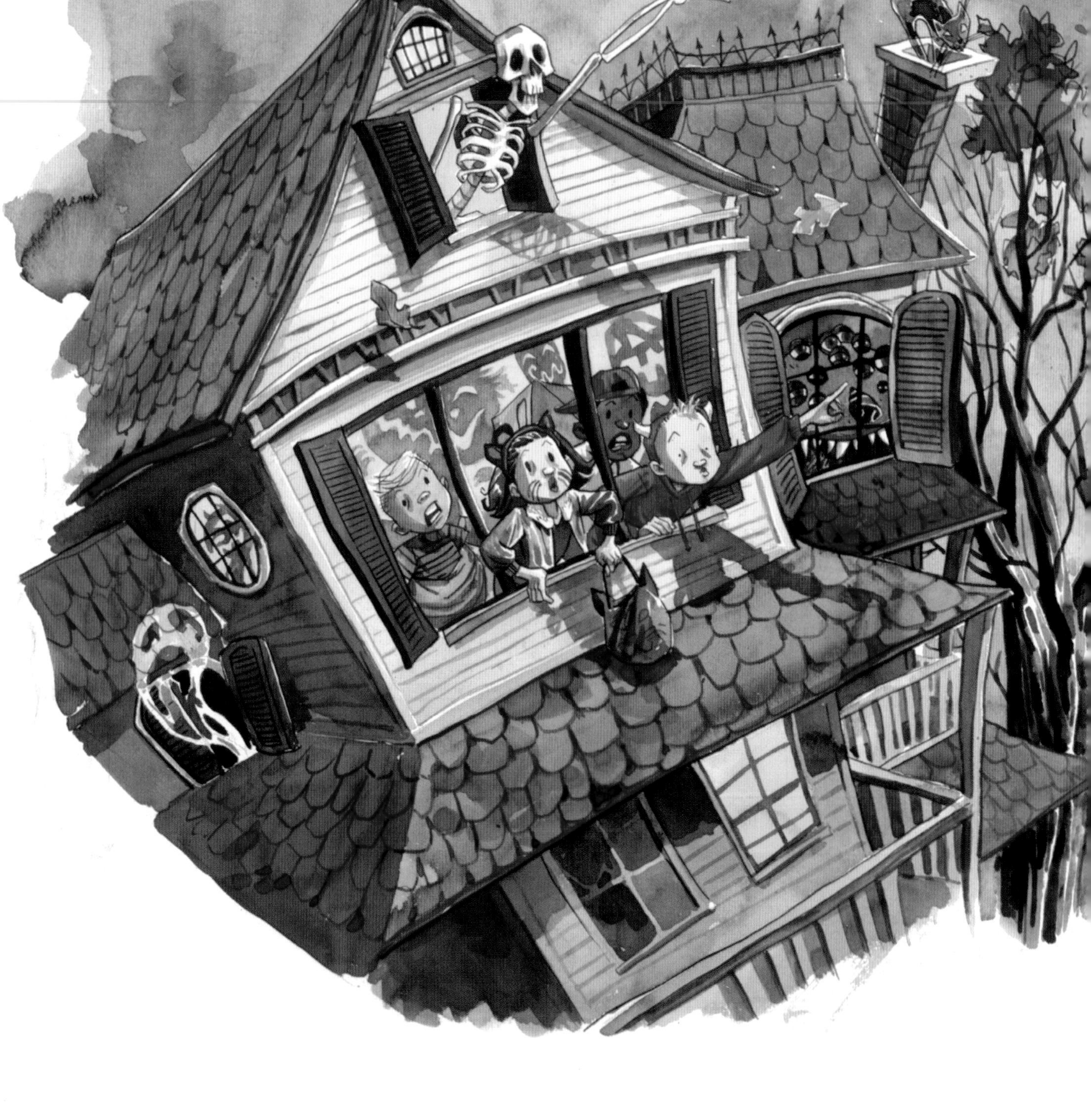

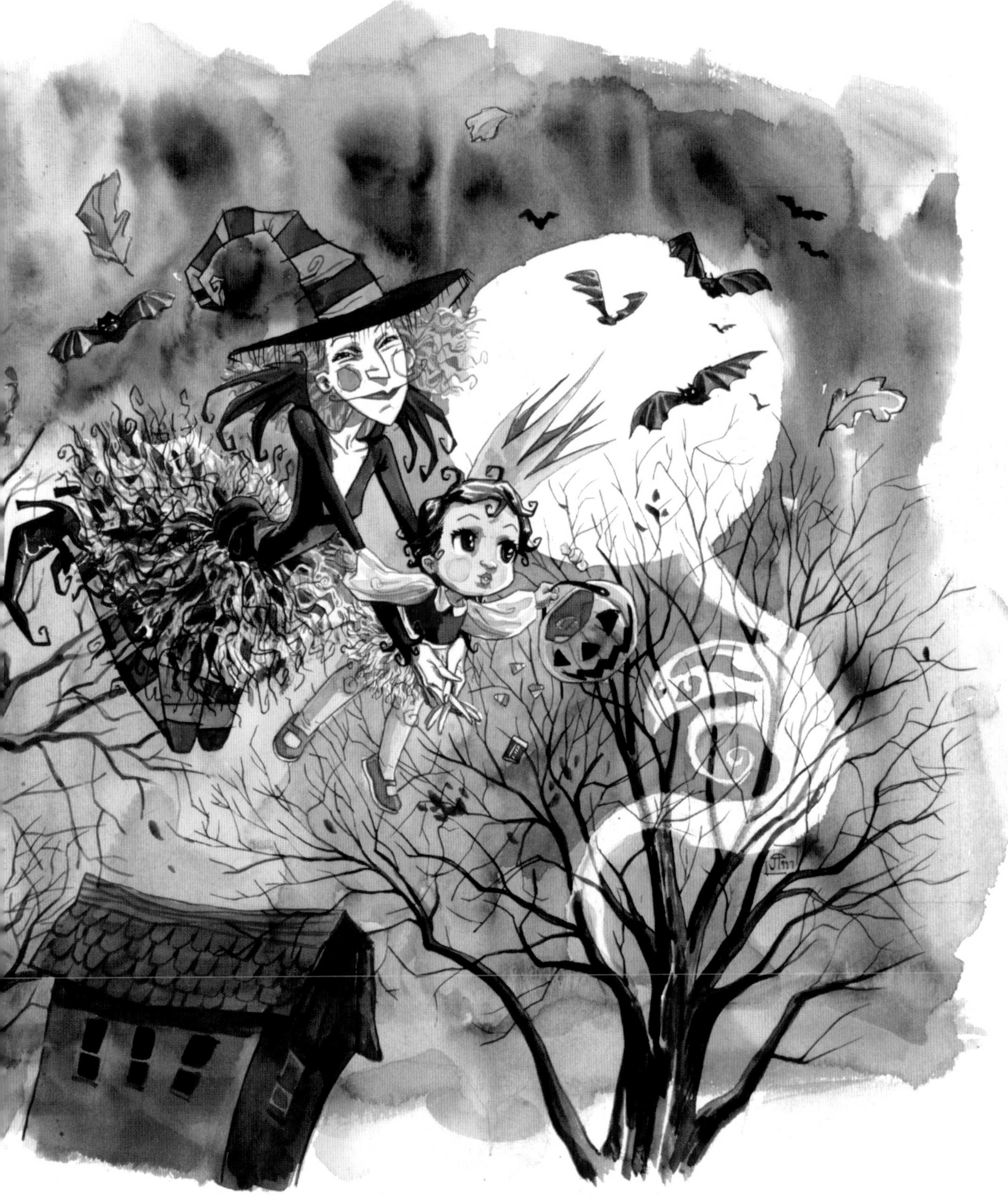

On the top left is the original black-and-white drawing of Bug-A-Boo. Creepy, yes. Cuddly, no. I needed more giant Muppet and less annoying goblin. Move your peepers over to the right. *Bingo!* Great Bug-A-Boo figures from his Mainframe expression sheet. On the top right is a page from *Scary Godmother* that I axed and redrew. I messed things up when I was working on the lettering. Above is a color turnaround of Bug-A-Boo.

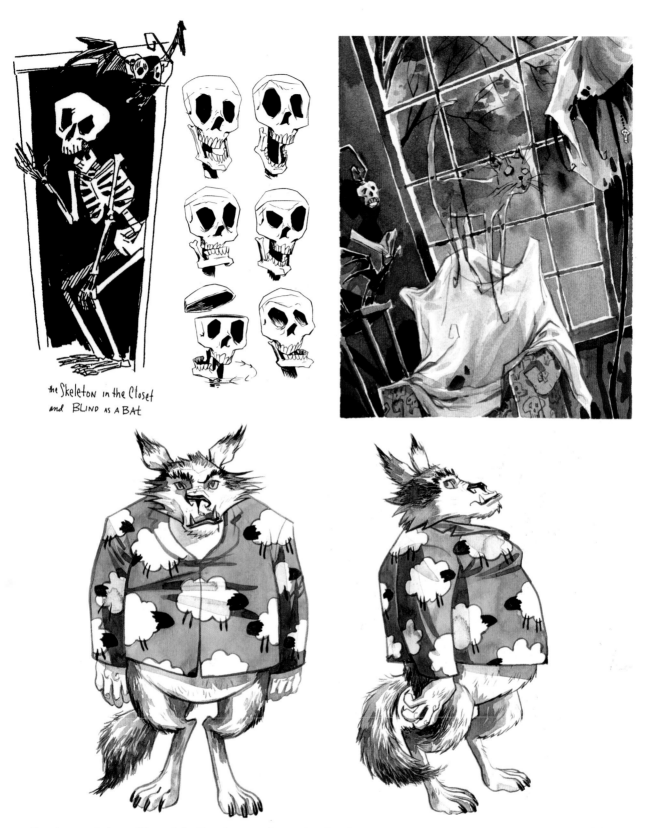

the Skeleton in the Closet
and BLIND as a BAT

On the top left you'll see Mr. Pettibone, who makes his first appearance on paper with "Blind as a Bat."
Skully didn't change at all, but there's not much you can do to alter a skeleton, now, is there?
Top right is a painting of the Boozle. Writer Will Pfeifer, who knew the real Boozle, named him!
Above is Harry the Werewolf, who is *thrilled* to appear in this turnaround!

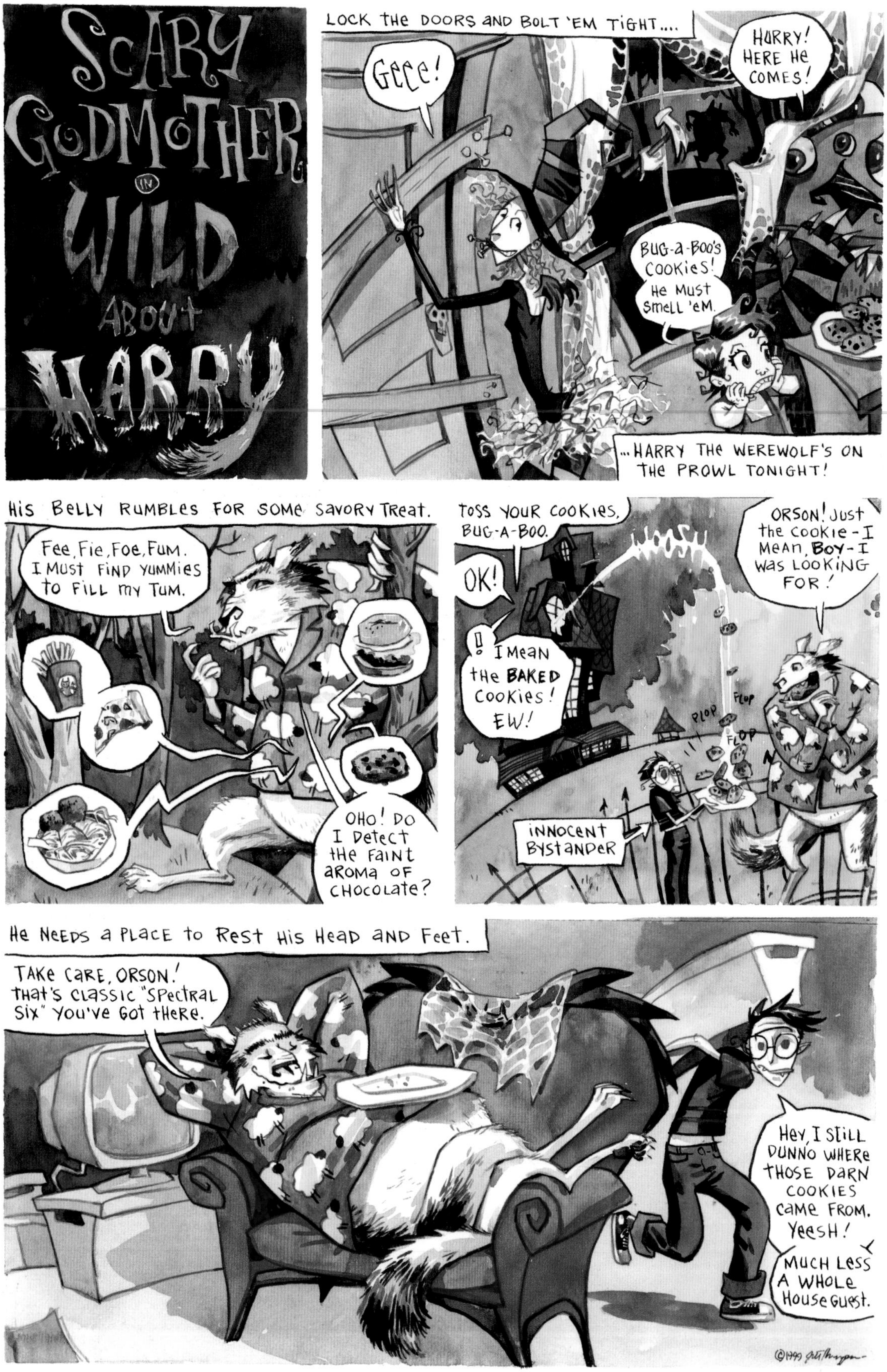

Scary Godmother in Wild About Harry
Lock the doors and bolt 'em tight....
Geee!
Harry! Here he comes!
Bug-a-Boo's cookies! He must smell 'em.
...Harry the werewolf's on the prowl tonight!
His belly rumbles for some savory treat.
Fee, Fie, Foe, Fum. I must find yummies to fill my tum.
Oho! Do I detect the faint aroma of chocolate?
Toss your cookies, Bug-a-Boo.
OK!
! I mean the BAKED cookies! EW!
WHOOSH
PLOP
FLOP
FLOP
Orson! Just the cookie - I mean, Boy - I was looking for!
innocent bystander
He needs a place to rest his head and feet.
Take care, Orson! that's classic "Spectral Six" you've got there.
Hey, I still dunno where those darn cookies came from. Yeesh!
Much less a whole houseguest.

And speaking of Harry, here we have a rhymey ad I did to publicize the *Scary Godmother* comic miniseries titled *Wild About Harry*. Also, one of the many Harry expression sheets I provided to the animators at Mainframe. Harry was quite popular and had a wide range of expressions for such a canine fellow!

On top we've got the credits illustration for *The Revenge of Jimmy*,
followed by the wraparound cover! I love that cover!

The front and back cover illustrations for *The Boo Flu* grace the top of this page, with
the wraparound cover for *The Mystery Date* tucked nicely underneath. What a fine line
I could command back then. Not so easy anymore. Alas, that paper is no longer available.
Yes, Jill, it must be all on account of the paper! Ha!

It's the vampire family! Yay! Max and Ruby form a heart-shaped embrace in an image from the set of valentine postcards produced by Sirius Entertainment in the late 1990s. You'll also see a few of the expressions and profiles for each of the vampires, which helped the animators at Mainframe gain an understanding of their posture and freakish proportions.

All of the valentine postcards.
I'm not sure if people bought them
to collect them, frame them, or
actually send them through the
mail, but I hope they sent them
through the mail!

I did many paintings while working on the animated specials with Mainframe Entertainment. All were used as reference by the animators and rendererers (yes, I spelled it that way on purpose). Some were used as backgrounds in the show itself, which was pretty freakin' incredible! They used the watercolor paintings to render the 3-D framing, making the backgrounds look both three dimensional and "Jill-painted" at the same time! Amazing! (Sorry for the lack of proper computer-animation terms. Analog gal here!)

So, we've got—on the top left side—the Spook House where the kids ditch Hannah, then below, the foyer of Scary Godmother's house, and some lanterns that were used to decorate her house for the Halloween party!

On the top left corner you'll see a view of Scary Godmother's living room, and to the right is the front door inside Scary Godmother's house. Below is a peek inside Belfrey Manor, the vampire family's castle, which we have not yet seen animated. Maybe one day! Still—nice digs, eh?

Above is the exterior of Hannah's house, based on the *real* Hannah's house (when she was a wee girl). Below is a shot of Hannah's neighborhood, and then the main drag on the Fright Side. You'll see the Gross-ery Store, the Comic Crypt sign, the Jack-o'-Lantern Diner, and cobblestone streets for the clip-clopping of horse-drawn carriages.

BLACKBIRD PIE
(FOUR AND TWENTY
OF COURSE)

CARAMEL APPLES
FINISHED WITH TINGE
OF CINNAMON SKY

GRAVEYARD
CAKES

CRISPY CRUNCHY
SNAKE SNAX

SWEET LADYFINGERS

TONGS FOR
SALAD

CHEEZ-TOES

DEVILS EGGS

ANT KRISPIE
SQUARES

BLOODY
MARY

GHOUL AIDE

SPICY BUFFALO
BATWINGS

WITH
CELERY
STIX &
BLUE CHEESE
DRESSING

HEAD CHEESE

NAME YOUR
POISON

SUGAR FRIED
INSECTS

Above, we have a veritable "boo-fay" of the treats that grace Scary Godmother's party table. Wouldn't you like to be a guest at one of her soirees? I can getcha the recipes!

On the following page, we close our sketchbook with the tipped-in bookplate Sirius did for the first Scary Godmother hardcover book. Ain't it sweet? C'mon, everybody, all together now . . . One, two, three—Awwww!

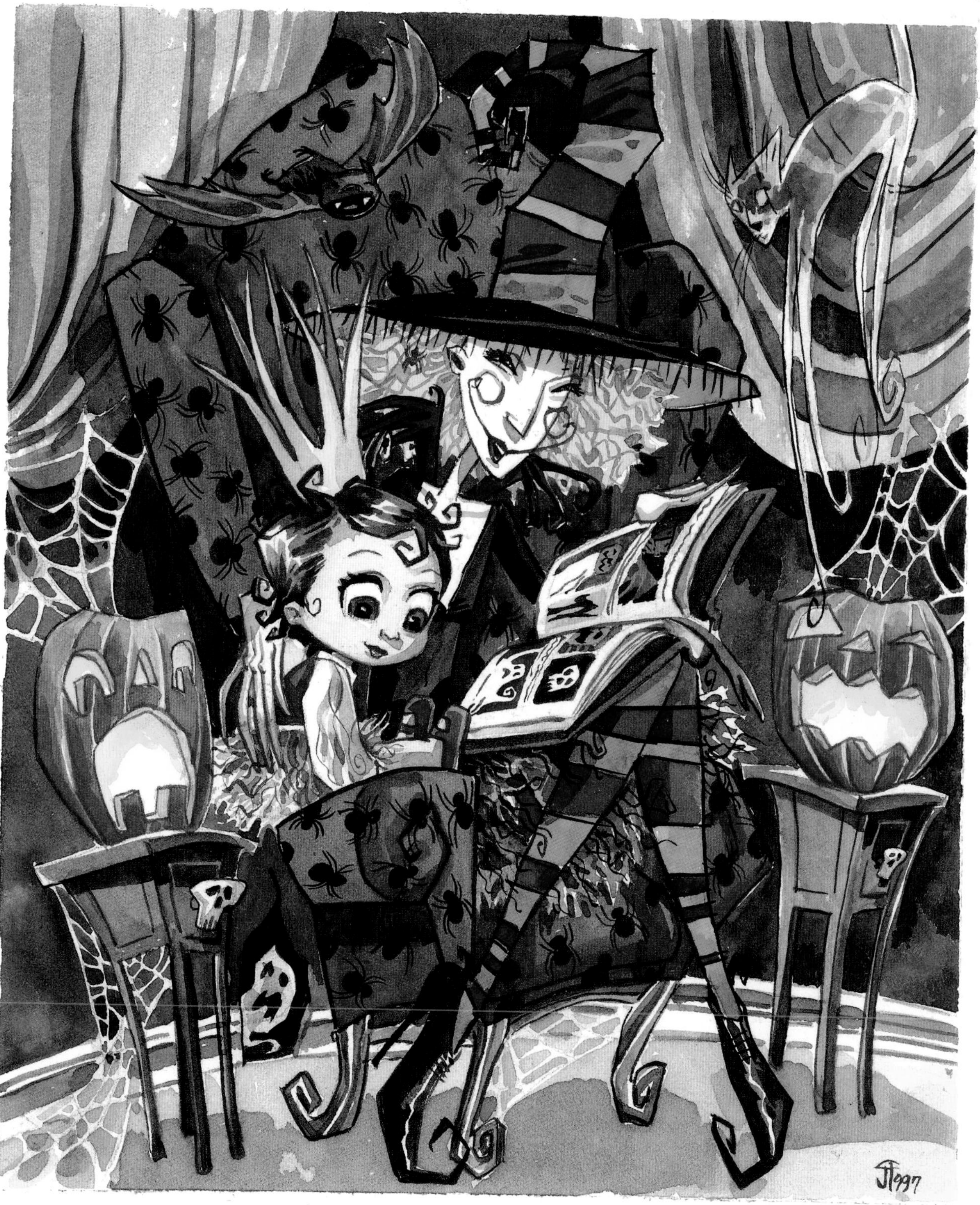

RECOMMENDED DARK HORSE READING . . .

*Plugtacular plugs! I heartily recommend you check these books out! Especially **Beasts of Burden** and **Sexy Chix**!*

BEASTS OF BURDEN VOLUME ONE: ANIMAL RITES
Evan Dorkin, Jill Thompson

Welcome to Burden Hill—a picturesque little town adorned with white picket fences and green, green grass, home to a unique team of paranormal investigators. Beneath this shiny exterior, Burden Hill harbors dark and sinister secrets, and it's up to a heroic gang of dogs—and one cat—to protect the town from the evil forces at work.

$19.99   ISBN 978-1-59582-513-1

SEXY CHIX
Jill Thompson, Joyce Carol Oates, Colleen Doran, and others

This time around the sexy chix in question are the writers and artists behind the comics, representing some of the best and brightest talent contributing to the medium of comics and graphic novels today. With stories ranging from mainstream adventures to hilarious comic shorts to heart-wrenching autobiography, *Sexy Chix* is devoted to the underrecognized contingent of female cartoonists in an overwhelmingly male-oriented industry.

$12.99   ISBN 978-1-59307-238-4

BUFFY THE VAMPIRE SLAYER SEASON EIGHT VOLUME ONE
Joss Whedon, Georges Jeanty

Since the destruction of the Hellmouth, the Slayers—newly legion—have gotten organized and are kicking some serious undead butt. But not everything's fun and firearms, as an old enemy reappears, Dawn experiences some growing pains, and one of the "Buffy" decoy slayers is going through major pain of her own.

$15.99   ISBN 978-1-59307-822-5

IT ATE BILLY ON CHRISTMAS
Roman Dirge, Steven Daily

It would have been a Christmas like any other for little Lumie and her horrible, terrible bully of a brother Billy. But then a little monster appeared and ate Billy right up! Lumie can't help but notice that things are much nicer now that he's gone. Now, Lumie has to decide what to do with her monster friend, and—most importantly—what she's going to *feed* him . . .

$12.99   ISBN 978-1-59307-853-9

AVAILABLE AT YOUR LOCAL COMICS SHOP OR BOOKSTORE
To find a comics shop in your area, call 1-888-266-4226. For more information or to order direct visit darkhorse.com or call 1-800-862-0052 • Mon.–Fri. 9 AM to 5 PM Pacific Time. *Prices and availability subject to change without notice.

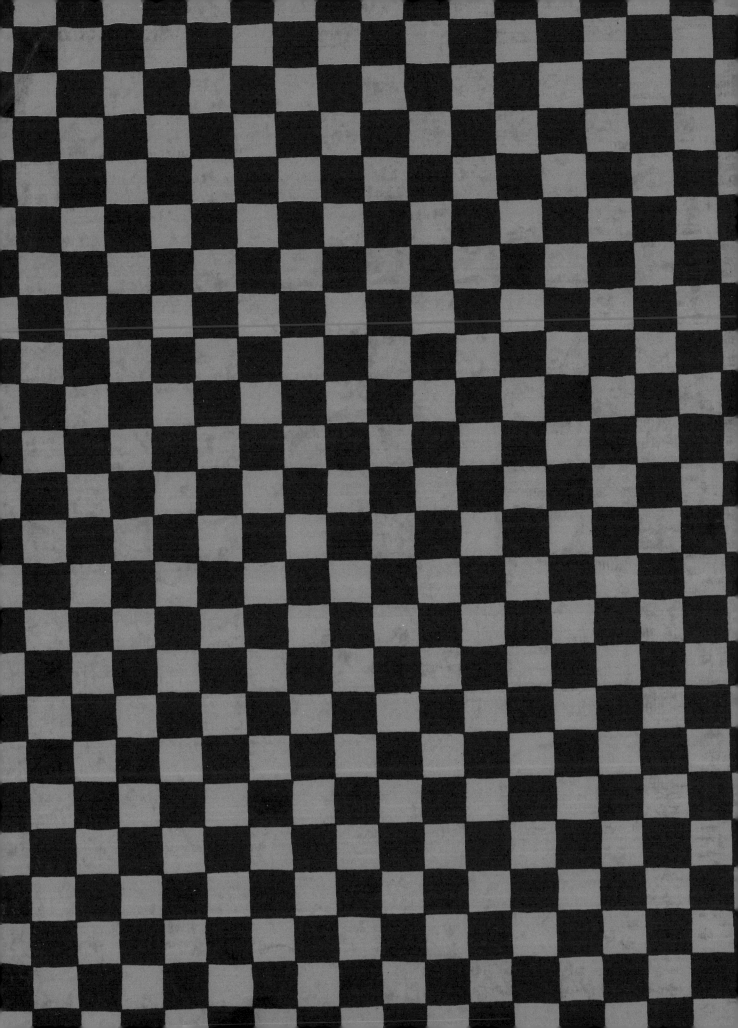